THE SEVEN HUNTERS WERE OVERHEAD . . .

"I have brought your pack."

"My pack?" Cartier asked.

"Yes." Pretty Weasel indicated the shapeless form on the ground. "I have put some meat in it, a few beads."

"But, Weasel, what—?"

"I am made to feel that you should find your son."

"But—"

Weasel held up his hand. "I will tell the marquis that I saw you, took over guard watch, and you started back to camp. I did not see you again."

Cartier sputtered in consternation.

"Woodchuck, you have been good to me. You spared my life, when most would have killed me. Now, I help you. Go home!"

The strange, unearthly thing about all this, Cartier realized numbly, is that it seems to make sense. Here is Weasel, whom I have known only a short while, encouraging me to desert my post, promising to cover for me, and the whole thing seems illogical. Hardly realizing what he was doing, Jean Cartier shrugged his shoulders into his pack. He glanced at the Seven Hunters and the Real-star, and started northwest with long strides. He did not pause until he reached the low crest of the ridge, then swung along a dimly lit trail.

Return to the River

>>>>>>>>>>

D O N C O L D S M I T H

BANTAM BOOKS
NEW YORK · TORONTO · LONDON · SYDNEY · AUCKLAND

All of the characters in this book
are fictitious, and any resemblance
to actual persons, living or dead,
is purely coincidental.

RL 6, IL age 12 and up

*This edition contains the complete text
of the original hardcover edition.*
NOT ONE WORD HAS BEEN OMITTED.

RETURN TO THE RIVER
A Bantam Book / published by arrangement with Doubleday

PRINTING HISTORY
Doubleday edition published September 1987
Bantam edition / July 1989

---

*Bantam Books are published by Bantam Books, a division of
Bantam Doubleday Dell Publishing Group, Inc. Its trademark,
consisting of the words "Bantam Books" and the portrayal of
a rooster, is Registered in U.S. Patent and Trademark Office
and in other countries. Marca Registrada. Bantam Books,
666 Fifth Avenue, New York, New York 10103*

---

*Time period: Middle seventeenth century.
Number 11 of the Spanish Bit Saga.*

Return
to
the
River
»»»»»»»»»»»

1

» » »

Captain Le Blanc was dissatisfied with the world. A few years ago he had dreamed great dreams, but these had turned to nothing. Here he was, caught in the back-eddy of the current of history, at a forgotten post on the frontier. A man could stagnate here.

His assignment at the apex of his country's thrust into the New World had looked exciting. Le Blanc fancied himself an explorer. He had postulated a water passage to the west, that elusive goal of both England and France. Somehow, he had become convinced that the long-sought waterway was not northwest, as most geographers thought, but *southwest*. There were maps which seemed to suggest this.

As commandant of the small frontier outpost Fort Mishi-ghan, Le Blanc had gone so far as to send an exploring party. It had been a secret mission, of course. He had no authority to take such a step. However, the covert nature of the mission had been a fortunate thing, as it turned out.

If the search had been successful, Le Blanc would have received acclaim as a far-sighted innovator. But it had been a dismal failure. The party had died in the unexplored wilderness, except for one man, who had brought back the tragic news.

One of the frontier's most promising young officers, André Du Pres, had been drowned on an unnamed river in the interior. Le Blanc had written a letter to the young man's parents, one of his most difficult tasks as commandant.

Also lost had been the half-breed scout Brûle, one of the most clever and experienced on the frontier.

Le Blanc had covered his tracks by reporting that they had been lost on a scouting trip. He had burned his carefully sketched maps, and managed to put at rest the theories and possibilities for exploration that might have made him famous as a discoverer. It was unfortunate that his gamble had failed, and that there had been loss of life.

Ah well, such were the risks of military service on the frontier. It could not be helped.

Still, the entire situation rankled within him. There was an entire continent out there to be explored and claimed in the name of His Majesty King Louis. Le Blanc was in a position to do so, but was prevented by circumstances. He could not free himself of the responsibility of the fort. If only he could lead an exploring party into the dangerous interior of the continent!

Or, as a second choice, send another party. True, his first attempt had been a disaster, one he had taken pains to conceal. But might not another expedition be more successful?

None of his superiors in the upper echelons of His Majesty's service knew of his fiasco. He had effectively concealed his error. Would it not be worth the risk to send another party? If someone under his command made a major discovery, gold, perhaps—he wandered in flights of fancy. The name Le Blanc might be as famous as that of the Spaniards Coronado and De Soto, or the Englishman Henry Hudson. The captain smiled to himself and tilted back in his chair to contemplate his dream world through half-closed eyelids.

Ah yes. He imagined himself among the aristocracy, telling tales of grandeur spiced with danger. Of course, he recounted to awestruck listeners. Of course we were in mortal danger nearly every day. We gladly suffered such risks in the service of the Crown. Yes, we planted the flag of France in the name of the King, in an area beset with danger but ripe with promise.

He was still tilted back in his chair, staring at the rough planks of the ceiling, when there was a knock at the door. Reluctantly, Le Blanc returned to reality.

"Yes, Lieutenant?"

He leaned forward and the front legs of the chair thumped hard against the wooden floor with a hollow sound.

"Sir," the young officer began apologetically as he entered the open door of the office, "a party is approaching."

"Natives?"

"No sir. French."

"On the trail? From which direction?"

"On the water, sir. Two canoes, perhaps eleven men."

Le Blanc leaped to his feet in alarm. For an instant, the thought crossed his mind that his secret had been found out, and that he was to be held responsible for the lives of the lost exploring party under his command.

"What is it, sir?" the astonished lieutenant blurted. "You are expecting trouble?"

"No, no," murmured the captain, regaining his composure and taking his blue tunic from the peg behind the chair. "But we must make them welcome."

A party approaching by water would be from the more established settlements to the northeast, along the chain of lakes. From civilization. Thus, for the forgotten outpost of Mishi-ghan, the newcomers represented authority. They might carry new orders, information, anything. Perhaps, even, he was to be transferred.

It seemed unlikely that the men in the canoes were

merely replacements or additional troops. Such missions would usually travel overland.

Therefore, Le Blanc reasoned, this must be a special mission of some sort. Possibly a reprimand, but more likely, merely a change of some sort in his command. Either way, Fort Mishi-ghan must look alive! He shrugged into his jacket and fumbled at the buttons.

"Lieutenant," he snapped, "take a platoon to greet them when they land. An honor guard. Which is the most efficient-looking?"

"Probably the Second Platoon, sir."

"Very well. Turn them out. I will meet them at the landing. Where is Lieutenant Le Croix?"

"In his quarters, I believe."

"Good. We must have this post presentable for inspection. Corporal," he called to the clerk at the desk outside his office, "have the drummer sound general quarters."

Le Blanc bolted out the door to stride toward the rustic building that housed the officers' quarters. Behind him, the staccato beat of the drum began to rattle, and the post sprang to life. Soldiers trotted toward their assigned assembly points, buttoning tunics and buckling equipment as they ran.

The captain felt a glow of pride at the rapidity with which his troops mobilized. No matter who the leader of the newcomers might be, this display of preparedness was bound to impress him.

Close on the heels of this thought came another, in the form of a question. Who in the name of God could the visitor be, and what was his mission?

2

» **»** **»**

Captain Le Blanc could hardly believe his eyes as the big canoes moved in to nose gently against the bank. A man leaped quickly from the prow of each vessel to drag it farther ashore.

The source of Le Blanc's astonishment was the second man in the nearest canoe. From his demeanor and bearing, this man was apparently the leader of the party. Yet, he would have appeared more at home in an elegant ballroom or at court. His clothing was immaculate, and Le Blanc wondered for a moment how he was able to appear so fresh and well groomed while traveling.

The stranger rose and stepped shakily forward in the canoe. His powder blue suit still seemed oddly out of place, with the lace cuffs of a highly styled shirt protruding conspicuously at the wrists. As the man stood, Le Blanc saw below the knees white hose, which reached from the gathered pale blue pantaloons to shiny black slippers on his feet. His hat, matching the blue of the tunic and trousers, was decorated with a long, fluffy ostrich plume. His powdered wig seemed ludicrous on the frontier.

Mon dieu, thought Le Blanc, what is this? A pampered, foppish dandy. What can he want here?

His heart sank as he anticipated the problems that this guest could cause. There was no way that the frontier post could possibly extend the civilities to which this young aristocrat was obviously accustomed. The man's entire person exuded a confidence that said he was a nobleman. He undoubtedly expected to be waited on, hand and foot, as he had been all his life. A twinge of resentment flickered in the captain's mind, and he quickly tried to squelch it.

The newcomer jumped nimbly from the canoe, and returned Lieutenant Le Croix's salute with a casual wave. He strode past the stiffly arrayed Second Platoon, up the slight slope toward the place where Le Blanc waited.

The captain had a moment to evaluate the young nobleman as he walked. Rather handsome, in an effeminate way. The eyes, wide-set above strong cheekbones, roved quickly to take in the surroundings. A carefully waxed moustache tapered to needle-sharp points at each side.

Perhaps the most unexpected thing about the newcomer, however, was the way he moved. His walk was one of catlike grace, a smooth, flowing motion that seemed effortless. It was reminiscent of the power in a coiled spring, ready to snap into action at a second's notice. Or, more accurately, perhaps, like the potential in the cold steel of a rapier. Slender and flexible as a willow wand, such a weapon was designed for a deadly thrust at any instant that it became necessary.

Mon dieu, thought Le Blanc again, I have almost misjudged this man.

Far from the pompous, effeminate dandy that he appeared at first glance, this was a man to be reckoned with. He could be dangerous. Not only politically dangerous, but in the area of martial skills. Simply from the way he moved, Le Blanc was certain that the newcomer was expert with the fencing foils. And hence, with the rapier, the captain finished the simile in his mind.

"Good day, *mon capitaine*."

6

The newcomer smiled, a disarming smile that showed even white teeth beneath the stylish little moustache.

"Welcome, monsieur." Le Blanc saluted and then extended his hand in greeting. "We are honored."

"Yes, yes, of course," the other responded with a casual wave of his hand. "You are Captain Le Blanc?"

"Yes, monsieur, commandant here at Fort Mishi-ghan." The newcomer nodded in satisfaction.

"Very well. I am Pierre, Marquis de Foixainne. Come, we must talk. Do you have some brandy?"

"Certainly. Let us go to my office."

He turned, gestured to the lieutenant to dismiss the honor guard, and started up the slope to the log stockade.

"Has your journey gone well?"

"Yes. Very exciting, this country. We came from Quebec, then through the lakes. Very impressive. Very."

The glitter of excitement in the eyes of the marquis showed that this was not idle conversation. The interest was there.

"You encountered no English?"

"No." The newcomer shook his head. "Too far north, I am told."

Le Blanc nodded. He still had no inkling as to this man's purpose here. His stomach stirred uneasily with a gnawing doubt. They crossed the compound, past groups of sharply uniformed soldiers lounging at ease, but ready to respond to command. Le Blanc led the way through the outer room and stepped aside to gesture the visitor into his office.

"Close the door, please," said the marquis over his shoulder.

Le Blanc did so, and then drew two glasses and a bottle from a drawer. He poured the amber liquid and extended one to the other man. The marquis took the glass, sniffed the aroma as he swished the brandy gently around, and then raised the vessel in a salute.

"To New France!"

"New France," echoed Le Blanc.

Still, he had no inkling as to what this was all about. The brandy burned his throat, and its aromatic fumes rose through the back of his nostrils to spread their mellow effect to his eyes and brain. He would find out, he decided, what the purpose of the visit was, when the marquis was ready.

Le Blanc sipped his brandy again. The visitor was now reaching into an inside pocket of his coat. He drew out a parchment-wrapped packet and opened it to take out a letter. The captain could see, even across the room, that there was a very official-looking seal attached.

"My letter of marque," said the visitor simply, extending the document to Le Blanc.

The captain scanned it quickly. It was simply a letter of authorization, permission to cross enemy lines if necessary, and a request that the bearer be given every assistance. At the bottom was affixed the Royal Seal of Louis XIII.

Le Blanc carefully refolded the commission and handed it back.

"Yes, monsieur, how may I help you? What is your mission?"

"Exploration, Captain," he whispered.

The eyes of the marquis glittered with excitement.

Le Blanc's heart beat faster. Perhaps this was his chance of a lifetime. He was not only rubbing shoulders with those close to royalty, but with a man who had dreams and goals like his own. If only he had not panicked and burned all his maps! He must be cautious, however.

"The Northwest Passage?"

"No, Captain," the other man chuckled. "That is like chasing a rainbow. Mine is a real mission."

"But what?" Le Blanc blurted.

He was thoroughly alarmed now. If this young nobleman wanted to go southwest, there could be a problem. Either Le Blanc must let him go, to enter dangerous unknown territory, or confide the truth. That he, Le Blanc,

8

had sent such a mission several years ago, which had perished.

"No." The marquis was smiling. "My mission is to find a river that is said to flow south, directly into the southern sea, the *golfo de México*. I am told you might know of such a river."

Now Le Blanc could relax. He began to see a way out of his dilemma. It was certainly better than nothing. Considerably better, even, than sitting here in New France's backwater, going nowhere. Le Blanc knew he could not go, personally, on this exciting mission. But there was one thing he could do, to enable him to bask in the reflected glory of anything the young explorer might discover.

"Monsieur." The captain almost purred. "I can certainly help your mission. I have a sergeant who has traveled partway down the Big River."

"Really?" The marquis was incredulous. "May I speak with him?"

"Of course."

Le Blanc rose and opened the door.

"Corporal, send me Sergeant Jean Cartier."

"Yes sir."

The captain turned and closed the door again.

"Monsieur," he smiled, "if it will help your mission, I will assign Sergeant Cartier to your party as guide."

3

» » »

Sergeant Jean Cartier was, of course, a bit apprehensive when he was summoned to the commandant's office. He knew something was in the wind.

Like everyone else at Fort Mishi-ghan, Cartier had seen the two canoes arrive at the landing. It would have been impossible *not* to know of their arrival. The sergeant, with the easy skill of a veteran soldier, had worked rapidly to help make the post presentable for visiting dignitaries. The visitors must be pleased, or at least appeased, with the appearance of the place. Then, soon, they would be gone, and the troops could return to their routine.

He had seen important visitors come and go for many years. The threat of their presence, the possibility of their displeasure, was a way of life in the military. It could be dealt with.

The object was to attract as little attention as possible, to blend with the ranks as a faceless entity, to be overlooked in the hectic events of the visitors' stay. To be sure, Sergeant Cartier had demanded that the men under him demonstrate a sharp, well-polished military appearance. Nothing excessive, of course. That would be self-defeating, would attract attention. It was better to appear good, but not best.

Not worst, either, of course. That would bring unpleasant attention sliding down the chain of command in the form of severe reprimand.

No, to sum up Cartier's philosophy of the military profession, one should be good but not best, and never volunteer for anything.

This trouble-free scheme had now been threatened. He had been summoned to the office of the captain, shortly after the visiting nobleman had accompanied Le Blanc inside.

Cartier had been visiting and joking with the men from the canoes, attempting to find out something about their mission. He had just discovered that it was some sort of exploratory thrust into the interior. This, in turn, made him more uneasy. The sergeant did not feel entirely comfortable about his part in the last exploratory expedition. Had his deception been discovered?

His anxiety mounted as he walked across the compound to present himself at the commandant's office. What if someone had discovered the real fate of the exploring party? He, Jean Cartier, could be in grave trouble. Perhaps he should have told the captain the truth in the first place. But no, he was certain that he had done right. There were many people involved. Enough to make Sergeant Jean Cartier feel that his decision had been the proper one. He still suffered pangs of remorse sometimes, over his falsification of a military report.

But the world had moved on. It seemed to have made little difference.

Now had come the strangers in authority, and a gnawing guilt had returned. Surely, they could not know.

He would play the game cautiously until he knew the way the wind was blowing. This was one more basic precept developed by the sergeant. If you don't know what's going on, say as little as possible until you find out.

He would find out in the first few minutes, Cartier believed. If he had really been caught in deception, one of the first events in the captain's office would be his arrest. With a cold chill on the back of his neck, the sergeant realized that he might even be charged with treason. That thought made him want to bolt and run, but it was too late now. He was already mounting the steps.

No, he decided. Such fears were ridiculous. If he was to be arrested, they would have sent someone to do so, not merely an unarmed messenger to request his presence.

Cartier nodded to the corporal at the desk, who casually jerked a thumb toward the captain's office. The sergeant stepped past the desk and through the open doorway. He saluted smartly.

"Sergeant Jean Cartier reporting as ordered, sir."

"At ease, Sergeant. And, please close the door."

"Yes sir."

Cartier quickly evaluated the situation. Only two men in the room, Captain Le Blanc and the marquis. Cartier relaxed somewhat. He would not have been called before these two just to be arrested. It must be something else.

"Sit down, please, Sergeant."

"Thank you, sir."

Le Blanc turned to the newcomer.

"This is the man, monsieur."

The words could have been alarming, but the captain's manner was reassuring. He was excited, but appeared unconcerned and happy.

"Yes, I see."

The marquis looked steadily at Cartier, sizing him up. Yet, even the stranger's bearing was reassuring. This look was one of interest, not displeasure or reprimand.

"You have been down the Big River, Sergeant?"

"Yes sir, for some distance," Cartier admitted cautiously. "Not to its mouth."

"Of course not," chuckled the marquis. "Tell me about the country."

Was this a trap of some sort? Cartier felt his palms become a trifle moist. He tried to remember how much he had falsified the actual facts. It was so long ago. No, he had primarily spoken of the land to the west in his report. This question was about the river country, not that beyond. Still, he must be careful, and not speak without thinking.

"Let me remember, sir," he began cautiously, watching for any change in facial expression. "Was it five, six years ago?"

"No matter, Sergeant. Tell the marquis what he wishes to know."

The captain's voice was crisp, a little harsh. It would not do to be too slow.

"Yes sir, of course. You wish to hear of the river country?"

"Yes, Cartier. How far south did you travel?"

"Well, it would be hard to say, sir. We capsized in a flood near the mouth of another big river, joining it from the west."

"Yes!" exclaimed the marquis excitedly. "We hear of the stream called the Big River by those in this area. I believe it is joined by other streams, and grows larger, farther south."

"Yes sir, it is as you say. At the point we wrecked, the river is several bow-shots across."

Immediately, he wondered if he had made an error. He had said "bow-shots," as his wife's people would say, instead of "furlongs," or other European units of measure. It was not known at the post that he had a native wife.

His thoughts wandered for a moment to the son he had left behind. Ground Squirrel, Pink Cloud had called the child. How difficult it had been to lose her. In his grief, he had fled the country of his bereavement. It had been the country of his greatest happiness, too, he now recalled. His eyes misted a little. Ground Squirrel would be six summers, now, probably learning the skills of the People in the Rabbit Society.

"Sergeant?"

The captain's voice seemed insistent.

"Oh. Yes sir?"

"I said, could you guide the exploring party of the marquis, here, down the Big River?"

"Of course, sir. I would be proud to do so."

The river. Just the river. They had not asked about the country beyond, to the west. That was the area of Cartier's deception. He had reported a desolate waste, peopled by savage beasts and savage tribes, too dangerous and too barren to bother with.

He had omitted mention of the abundant game and furs, and the lush grasses of the prairie that was the home of the People. And which had been his home, too, for a season.

At times, Sergeant Cartier could scarcely believe what he had done. He had falsified a military report, to spare his wife's people from the impact of civilization for a little while. It would be a long time before another expedition would be sent into the area.

Now this expedition was a different matter. They would travel on the river. He could not imagine the pampered nobleman, in his lace and finery, wishing to leave the comfort of his boats to travel overland. If they stayed on the Big River, there was no problem. The land of Pink Cloud's people, the Elk-dog People, was still far to the west, beyond the River of Swans.

4

» » »

Cartier had not confided to anyone since his return to Fort Mishi-ghan. How would it have been possible, even if he had wished to do so? How could he make anyone understand who had not been there? It was something that could not be described, but must be experienced. The wild sweep of the wind across the prairie, the great broad sky that reached from one horizon to the other. There was no way to tell anyone of the thrill of riding a good horse into a herd of buffalo, and accounting well for one's skill as a hunter. The warm feeling of exchanging congratulations with the other hunters, and the feasting that followed a successful hunt. No, he could not share these things.

Even less could he discuss his marriage to the beautiful Pink Cloud. There was no one at the post who could have understood the feelings he had had for her. Possibly Lieutenant Du Pres could know how he felt. Du Pres was still out there somewhere with the People, and his woman, Pale Star. They made as fine a couple as Cartier had ever seen. They had quickly become involved after the accident, when Star's husband was killed.

It had been one of those rare spontaneous romances that one sometimes sees, which seems to need no comment. It happens, and it seems that it was always so. It had been that way for Star and the lieutenant, and Cartier had envied them such a relationship.

Then he had found his own romance, in the person of Cloud, daughter of one of the band chiefs. The two couples had found a season of happiness that the sergeant had seldom imagined. The long days of the prairie autumn seeemed to promise that this existence could last forever.

Even the coming of winter had not been without some degree of pleasure. The two Frenchmen had been accepted by the tribe into which they had married. Du Pres, now known as Sky-Eyes, because of their unfamiliar blue color, was in great demand as a storyteller. As for himself, Cartier had expanded a knack for whittling into an art that gave him high esteem. Many of the People now carried a carved fetish or charm created by his skill. Woodchuck, he was called.

Cartier smiled to himself. It was a long time since he had thought of himself as Woodchuck. After the death of Cloud, he had wanted only to leave the memories behind. He had thrust himself back into the military routine, knowing that he was considered a trifle odd, but not caring. He frequently told himself that he had forgotten the season among the People, and that it was of no consequence. But he knew he lied to himself. He could never be the same person again.

Sometimes he wondered about Du Pres. Cartier had watched the young officer struggle with the conflict between duty and the love for his wife, her people, and their land.

When they had parted, the lieutenant was under the impression that his report would be delivered to the commandant. He had recommended exploration and settlement of the rich plains. But Cartier had burned the journal, unable to accept this disruption of the beautiful land that they had both come to love.

He had wondered sometimes what he would do if Du

Pres happened to return unexpectedly. He would plead innocence of any wrong, he supposed, implying that the oilskin-wrapped journal that he carried had been accidently destroyed. That was almost true.

Cartier had never quite figured out how to reconcile his story of Lieutenant Du Pres's death with the lieutenant's return, if it ever occurred. This had bothered him considerably for a year or two, but time had softened his worry. By this time, Du Pres would surely have returned to civilization if he intended to. Either that or he was dead. There were always risks and dangers involved in the vigorous life of the People.

The sergeant hoped that that was not the explanation. He held great affection for the lieutenant, and for his wife, without whom probably none of them would have survived. It pleased him more to think of the two of them, Sky-Eyes and Pale Star, as respected members of the tribe.

He wondered if they had a child yet. There had been a question, he recalled, whether Star could bear children. She had suffered physical and sexual abuse, when scarcely more than a child herself, and this was thought to be a contributing factor. He hoped that it had been possible for them.

The proudest experience of Cartier's life had been the birth of his son. His son and Pink Cloud's. The child was so young when the accident claimed her life, he would never remember his mother.

For perhaps the thousandth time, Cartier relived that awful moment when the wounded bull charged up out of a gully and so quickly snuffed the life of the gentle girl. Tears came to his eyes sometimes even now. He had been powerless to help her.

"Sergeant?"

"Yes. What?"

The corporal behind the rough plank counter in the store had caught him dreaming. *Mon dieu*, was he losing his mind?

17

"I said, Sergeant, will there be any other supplies for the marquis? Is that all the list?"

"I will tell you when I am finished!" blurted Cartier angrily.

He realized that his anger was from embarrassment, and wished he had not spoken so harshly. But there was no taking back the words now.

"That should be everything. You have the salt?"

The corporal nodded, somewhat cynically.

"Yes, Sergeant."

"Very well. We leave in the morning."

Inwardly, Cartier was concerned. He was finding himself increasingly prone to flights of fancy, since he had first heard of the expedition last night.

It had been a long time since he had allowed himself to think of some of the memories that now seemed to occupy his mind.

5

» » »

In the day prior to the expedition's departure, Cartier learned much about the young nobleman and his crew. Some of it was surprising.

Captain Le Blanc had ordered him to give full cooperation to the marquis, including suggestion and advice. Immediately, disagreements arose, but not in the areas Cartier had supposed.

He had expected, for instance, to have to argue that silks and lace were not appropriate to the frontier. To his surprise, the marquis had appeared the morning after his arrival in well-fitting buckskins that showed unmistakable evidence of familiar use. The finery, it appeared, was not only reserved for formal occasions, but the young man actually preferred buckskins. He had worn them, one of the party told Cartier, since they left Quebec, except for their brief visits to military posts.

The men who accompanied the marquis were specially selected, it seemed. They were neither soldiers nor sailors, were not even in the service of the Crown, but in the employ of the marquis himself. They were chosen for special skills, as boatmen and hand-to-hand fighters, a formidable force. Cartier knew that it was not uncom-

mon for privateers such as the marquis to employ mercenaries. This was his first close contact, however.

The marquis quickly made clear that Cartier's authority was second only to his own. Nonetheless, the sergeant
was impressed by the obvious expertise of the men
around him. He could learn much from these men.
"Voyageurs," the marquis called them. Cartier immediately felt the strong sense of confidence they had in each
other and their mission. He hoped he could gain their
respect and acceptance.

The first major problem arose when Cartier suggested
that they abandon the canoes and go overland to the Big
River.

"We can buy more at the river," he insisted.

It was obvious that cost was no object. However, the
marquis firmly refused to consider such advice.

"*Mon dieu,* no!" he almost shouted. "These are special
canoes, made for us at Quebec. We cannot leave them.
We will carry them!"

Feeling chastised, Cartier still felt that the other did
not understand.

"But, Excellency, it is many days by land to the Big
River!"

"So be it," the marquis shrugged. "We carry them."

Still not convinced, Cartier went to inspect the craft.
They were, indeed, superior in workmanship. The sergeant was most familiar with the common canoes of the
area, built to accommodate two or three people and baggage. Often they were used by one.

These, on the other hand, were the larger type, designed to carry six to eight. "War canoes," they were
called by the tribes of the area.

"You see, monsieur," one of the voyageurs was ex-
plaining to him, "these are of special design. The marquis
had them built to his specifications."

It was nothing readily seen by the eye. A slight difference in the taper of the prow and the stern, a minor
change in the ratio of length to beam. Overall, the fragile

construction had been maintained, to keep weight to a minimum.

"Does it work well?" Cartier asked candidly.

"But of course, monsieur," the voyageur insisted. "Not quite as fast on a straight run, perhaps, but more stable. Less draught."

"Draught?"

"Yes," the other man chuckled. "I forgot, you are not a sailor. These canoes are broader, so they do not sink as deeply into the water, no?"

"I see. Do they maneuver well?"

"Well enough. We will not use them for fighting, only for travel."

Satisfied on that point, Cartier still had doubts.

"But how are they to carry?"

"Three men can carry one well."

Quickly, Cartier considered. Three to carry each canoe. That would leave only six to carry the considerable amount of baggage, even if the marquis carried a share. For a short journey on level ground, it might suffice. For the many days required overland to the Big River, he had his doubts.

Would it be possible, he wondered, to hire local natives to carry, at least part of the way? Close on the heels of this, another thought struck him. There were many small streams to the south, all presumably flowing southwest, converging and ultimately emptying into the Big River. Perhaps the overland trek to one of these streams would be shorter than the trail west, directly to the river.

"Tell me," he inquired of the voyageur, "what happens when you come to a shallow place, or rapids, or a waterfall?"

"We portage. Pick up the canoes and go around."

They returned to the fort, where Cartier quickly outlined his idea to the marquis. Then the two went to Le Blanc's office to study the maps on the wall.

"Yes, here!" exclaimed the marquis excitedly.

He poked a finger at a stream to the south.

"We could put in here. There is a trail?"

"Yes, Excellency. We do not use it much."

"Our patrols do not range that far," contributed Le Blanc.

"How far?"

"That is four, maybe five sleeps," answered Cartier.

He paused, startled that he had used the native term rather than the European expression of distance. The marquis seemed not to notice. He was enough of a frontiersman to understand the reference.

"Maybe six, with our baggage and canoes?"

"Yes sir. But perhaps we can hire local natives to carry."

"Very well. But the canoes must be carried by the voyageurs."

Cartier understood this precaution. The craft were easily damaged. If a canoe happened to be dropped, it could be hurt beyond repair. He nodded agreement.

"The voyageurs might trade off frequently, if the baggage is carried by others."

"Good thought, Sergeant," Captain Le Blanc approved.

The marquis nodded.

"Can you find some natives?"

"Yes sir. I think so. I will go now, to hire some, if you wish."

"Very good, Sergeant. Tell them we start at dawn."

6
» » »

The chill of the foggy morning made him think inescapably of that other journey's start, years before. Captain Le Blanc came out to see them off, as before, and Cartier had the eerie feeling that he had lived this day before.

There were differences, of course. They were starting on the little-traveled trail to the south, rather than the broad path to the west. The party was larger, more defensible against attack. The bulk of the canoes, carried upside down over the heads of the voyageurs, was unfamiliar. So was the amount of baggage and supplies. The marquis intended to be well supplied with trade goods.

One marked similarity struck him as he shouldered his pack. He knew none of his companions. That part was exactly like before, except more so. On the first mission, he had only a speaking acquaintance with the scout Brûle, his wife, and Lieutenant Du Pres.

Brûle was dead now, drowned in the Big River. Du Pres had become his best friend. Yes, a friend. They had been more than fellow soldiers, despite their difference in rank. Closer than brothers. They were fellow warriors of the People, he thought, and was immediately startled again at himself. Strange, how this present series of events was making him recall that other part of his past. It now seemed a lifetime away, part of another world.

He wondered about his son. Ground Squirrel, he had been called as an infant. It had been a joke. The child resembled his father, some thought, and is not a ground squirrel like a very small woodchuck?

The boy would have another name, now. It would have been bestowed at his First Dance, at age two. The name would have been chosen by his grandfather, Red Feather, most likely. How strange, Cartier thought, not to even know the name of his son.

He had left the child in the keeping of Pale Star when he left the People. Here he knew there would be the best care it was possible for them to provide. Later, at the Big Council, Star may have turned the baby over to his grandparents, who were of a different band.

Cartier had not wondered much about this. He had only wanted to forget. Now, with this journey bringing back memories of the other, questions kept occurring to him. Who *had* raised the baby? Was he strong and healthy? Was he adept with the throwing sticks and the other childish skills of the Rabbit Society? Was he learning the use of the bow? Was he liked and respected by the other children?

These questions ultimately had led to the others, those which nagged at his subconscious and had bothered his night's sleep. What did the youngster know of his father? He would have been too young, of course, to remember, but what had been told him? Whoever had raised the baby would have told him about his mother, and how she had been killed. But what had been said about his father? And why, when it came down to it, should he, Cartier, even care? He would never see the child again.

Cartier glanced around. The hired pack carriers were ready to shoulder their packs. The voyageurs lounged near the canoes, which had been carried up the steep slope from the lake.

Captain Le Blanc and the marquis stood talking, and Cartier sauntered over to where they waited.

"Ready, sir?"

"Yes, Sergeant, whenever you say. You will lead, no?"

"Yes sir, at least for now. We may need local guides somewhere."

"Of course."

"Excellency," spoke the captain effusively, "may your journey be a profitable one."

"Thank you, Captain. We shall hope so. I appreciate all your help, and the loan of Sergeant Cartier as a guide."

"It is nothing. Glad to be of service."

"Sergeant," continued Le Blanc, almost too warmly, as he shook Cartier's hand, "bring me as accurate a report as on your last journey, but hopefully, more optimistic."

Feelings of guilt flooded over Cartier as he smiled self-consciously.

"Yes sir."

"You are assigned to His Excellency, the marquis, as long as he has need of your assistance."

"Yes sir."

Cartier saluted, then turned and started toward the path that led into the fog. He paused to watch the voyageurs lift the canoes to carrying position.

Three men stood beside the craft, facing the rear. Together, they bent and each placed his hands to grip the edges of the shell at the sides.

The man in the rear gave terse commands.

"Une, deux, trois!" he barked.

On the count of three, they lifted and turned as one, now facing forward and with the big canoe upside down over their heads. Cartier had seen this maneuver before, but not with such crisp efficiency. The voyageurs were certainly well disciplined.

He strode toward the trail, and the marquis fell into step beside him. He could hear grunts as the pack carriers shouldered their burdens and fell into line.

The other canoe was lifted to the rhythmic cadence,

"une, deux, trois," and the party straggled out onto the trail.

It seemed only moments before the morning fog closed behind them and they were traveling in the emptiness of another world. Cartier hoped that the overland portage would prove to be a good idea. So far, they seemed to be moving well.

They stopped some time later in response to a call from the rear. The voyageurs wished to change carriers. It was an opportunity to walk up and down the line and check on progress. Everything seemed to be going well.

"It is good," observed Cartier, unconsciously using in French an expression often voiced by the People in their own tongue.

The marquis, at his elbow, grunted agreement. The rising sun to their left was just beginning to burn away the shadows of the night and scatter the fog as they prepared to move on.

7

» » »

It did not take long for Cartier to gain great respect for the voyageurs of the marquis. Here were skilled mercenaries, hand-picked men who knew their jobs. Where he had harbored some doubts about the advisability of carrying the two big canoes, he was now convinced.

He was pleasantly surprised to find that their progress was much faster than he had feared. By the second day, the rhythm of travel was established. Camp for the night, start on the trail, pause to trade carriers, resume travel. The natives hired as pack carriers were performing well, too.

Their travel was somewhat less complicated by the fact that there were no hostile forces in the area. At least, Cartier thought not. To the north or west, there would be the confusion of loyalties, which tribe was allied with whom, and where they might be. Some tribes and individuals had no firm loyalties. They wavered from French to English and back like the changing wind, depending on which side seemed to be paying best at the moment.

Here, on their present trail, there should be no problem. The tribes here were well known, and if not pro-French, were at least neutral. Yes, this was probably a better way to reach the water than the usual trail to the west, to the Big River.

If they were free from the threat of ambush, as their native pack carriers insisted, their journey could be planned with more freedom. Of course, it seemed only prudent to post a watch each night.

Cartier's main concern was that he was in unfamiliar territory. He was supposed to be guiding the party, but at the outset he had suggested this overland portage through an area unknown to him.

"How much farther to the river, Sergeant?" the marquis had asked on the third evening.

"Monsieur, you must understand this is a new trail to me, too," Cartier pleaded. "We will come to a stream somewhere in this direction. All these streams flow southeast, eventually into the Big River."

"Ah yes, I understand."

"We might ask the natives."

He rose and walked over to the fire where the leader of their hired carriers squatted.

"Small Bear," he asked, "do you know how far to the first stream?"

The man gave a grunt that seemed to be an assent to the question, and continued to smoke in silence. Cartier waited, amused. This sort of response, so typically native, was a matter of extreme frustration to some of the Europeans. He had once found it so, himself. Gradually, living with the People, he had come to understand. It was considered impolite to answer a question that has not been asked.

Hence, when he had asked Small Bear "do you know," the other had nodded "yes." Having answered the question, he lapsed into silence.

"Well?" the marquis asked impatiently.

Cartier waited a moment longer, a polite interval that would not be lost on Small Bear.

"How far?"

The man removed the pipe from his lips and exhaled a fragrant cloud as he looked up at the sergeant.

"Maybe two sleeps."

"It is good."

Cartier turned to the marquis and relayed the information in French.

"He says about two days, monsieur."

"Good! Then we make better time than expected, no?"

"Yes, perhaps. It goes well."

"And we are not likely to meet any hostile natives?"

"I think not, monsieur. We can safely travel for the present. After we start the river portion of the journey, there may be local situations unknown to us."

The marquis nodded.

"Of course. But on your previous journey, you encountered no hostility?"

Be careful now, Cartier told himself. The story must be as near the truth as possible, but stop short of the whole story. He had reported dangerous savages to Captain Le Blanc.

"Monsieur, it is hard to say," he answered cautiously. "Our expedition was destroyed on the river. Some of the local natives helped me to survive and to recover."

"You were injured?"

"Not injured, really. Half drowned."

Cartier was becoming uncomfortable. He wondered how much the marquis knew of the time involved. How could he account for the year that they had spent, far to the west, after the accident? Beyond the River of Swans, as far as the shadow of the great mountains, the People had traveled while he was one of them. Would the marquis notice that missing year?

"So the local tribes helped you?" the marquis was asking.

"Yes, monsieur. I stayed with them for a while. They were river people. They spoke of dangerous tribes farther west."

There, that should do it. He would try to say very little more.

"I see. Tell me, Sergeant, how were you able to communicate? Is the language the same as that of these natives?"

"No, monsieur. There are many languages. They all use the sign talk."

"Ah yes. I have seen this in use. All tribes use it?"

"More so to the west, and on the river."

"How did you learn?"

"The wife of the scout, Brûle, who was lost in the accident, taught us, as we traveled."

"It would be useful for me to learn?"

Cartier paused before answering. He liked this young nobleman, and his eagerness to learn the ways of the frontier. Still, there were advantages if the marquis did not know too much. The sergeant struggled with his conscience a moment, and his basic honesty won out.

"Yes, monsieur, it would," he said slowly.

"Could you teach me?"

"Yes, I suppose so."

"Good. When do we begin?"

"At once, if you wish."

The marquis nodded.

"Proceed."

"Yes, monsieur. Mostly, it is simple signs. To start, here is 'water.' "

He made a horizontal flowing motion with the fingers of one hand, palm down.

"This, 'eat.' A finger pointed into the mouth. A finger out from the mouth is 'talk.' "

The marquis nodded, trying the signs as they were explained. Small Bear looked up, interested. Cartier noticed, and paused to explain.

"The white chief wishes to learn the sign talk."

The other grunted.

"It is good," he signed.

Cartier turned back to the marquis.

"Small Bear says it is good," he explained. "That was the sign for approval."

"His people use sign talk?"

"Not as much as farther west. Most of them know a little of it."

"How do I sign 'thank you'?"

"You can use the sign that he just used. It is agreement or approval. 'It is good' would be a good answer."

"It is good," signed the marquis to Small Bear.

A broad grin split the dusky face, and the man nodded, pleased.

"This one can go far," he said in his own tongue. "It is good, Woodchuck."

Late that night, Cartier sat staring into the coals of the campfire. It was good, to be in buckskins again. He had forgotten how comfortable such garments were.

With the return to buckskins had come a strange transformation. He began to remember things from the past, from his season on the prairie. The glowing fire flickered and cast shadows against the trees at the edge of the clearing. A night bird called, and its mate answered. From somewhere in the distance came the hollow call of *Kookooskoos*, the great hunting owl.

The night lacked only the cry of the coyote to remind Cartier of the open prairie and the wide sky. It would be good, he thought, to hear the coyote song again. Perhaps the deeper call of the lobo wolves as they followed the herds of migrating buffalo.

Mon dieu, he asked himself, why am I thinking these things? One might think I was homesick.

He stirred the fire and tossed some partly burned sticks into the hotter portion of the embers. Tiny tongues of flame danced and sputtered, and the coals seemed alive. He stared, hypnotized, his thoughts a world away. What was it that Looks Far had once said? A man sees pictures of his past in the embers of his fire.

The medicine man had been one of the most intelligent people he had ever met, thought Cartier. He had not thought of Looks Far for a long time. He had been, he now realized, trying to escape his sorrow by refusing to look at that part of his life.

It had been successful, after a fashion, he supposed. It was not until now, again on the eve of travel into the unexplored reaches of the continent, that that forgotten life came crowding back into his consciousness. On that other journey, during the evening camps, Pale Star had taught them the sign talk. That had been a valuable skill later. Now, in turn, he was teaching the marquis, leader of a new exploring party.

Of course, Cartier told himself, there was hardly a parallel. This mission would travel down the Big River to its mouth. He would be seeing new territory from the point where they had capsized. They would never come close to the River of Swans and the memories beyond.

His natural curiosity made him wonder as to the lower river, and the point where it emptied into the southern sea. It would be good to see new sights, experience new smells and sounds.

Yes, this expedition might well remove the memories, and put the old feelings to rest. It would be better when they began to travel on the Big River, the "Father of Rivers."

He distracted his thoughts by thinking again of the expedition. It was going well, there could be no doubt of that. But what if, he thought, what if they did encounter hostile natives unexpectedly?

He had, without making a point of it, attempted to evaluate the weapons of the party. The marquis, as he had somehow expected, wore a slim, efficient-looking rapier. It seemed out of place against the buckskins of the frontier, but Cartier did not question its effectiveness. At his right side, the marquis also carried a throwing-ax, as well as a belt knife. Cartier somehow had no doubt that the young nobleman would be equally proficient with all three.

The voyageurs carried an assortment of weapons. At first, Cartier had assumed that the selection was based on individual preference, because it was seemingly so random. Yet, there appeared to be a pattern. Six of the men carried muskets. The sergeant had little regard for this unreliable specialty weapon, but it was probably well to have a few along. It was the second day before he realized something. In the course of travel, the musketeers always seemed to trade off so that there were two carrying canoes and four walking with muskets at hand. Two were always near each canoe.

He had heard no command to this effect. It simply seemed to happen. By the next day, he had observed the voyageurs enough to realize that this was standard procedure, carried out as expected. Again, he marveled at the deadly efficiency of these men.

The rest of the party carried belt knives or throwing-axes, or both. He noted that some of the knives were of the heavy frontier pattern. Others, however were wicked-looking fighting knives, with slim double-edged blades and rounded tapering handles. Dirks, he had heard this style called.

Normally, a platoon of this size would have included pikemen, and Cartier wondered for a moment at their absence. Then he realized that pikes would be very difficult to carry in a canoe. Besides, in any fighting they happened to encounter, pikemen would not be a particular advantage.

One man, a quiet introspective individual, wore an old-fashioned short crossbow slung over his back. A quiver of wicked-looking bolts for the weapon hung at his waist. Cartier gathered, from the deference the others showed this man, that his ability was well respected. He was somewhat older than the others, and his entire demeanor reflected experience. He was called simply "the Bowman." Cartier gathered that he had been with the marquis for some time, perhaps a family retainer.

As for the sergeant himself, he had without thinking reverted to the weapons of his time on the prairie. He carried the short, stout bow of the native hunter, a supply of arrows, and an ax and knife at his belt.

He had not used the bow since his return to civilization. It had hung over his bunk, hardly noticed. Now, as he carried the weapon, it seemed familiar to his hand. He could recall the thrill of success in the hunt, the congratulations of the other warriors as they counted the kill and the butchering parties straggled over the ridge to begin work.

"A good hunt, Woodchuck! You have three kills?"

Cartier smiled to himself in the darkness. It had been good, that season. The memories were saddened only by the fact that among those coming to begin the skinning and preparing of the meat would have been Pink Cloud.

It was not unusual, he supposed, that he would miss her more tonight. Here at a wilderness campfire, in the native dress of her people, with the night sounds around him, she seemed close.

There was comfort in the way he felt. Despite the sadness in the memories, there was optimism, somehow. There were more good memories than bad. He took a deep breath. Could it be that he was beginning to recover from his loss? Or was he just now beginning to allow the spiritual forces, the "medicine" of the People, to come to his assistance? Or, he wondered, was it much the same thing? He wished for a moment that he could talk to Looks Far.

It was no matter, he decided finally. He would never see Looks Far again, but at least he was feeling better. Better about the world, his place in it, and his present mission. Something was going right, for the first time since he left the People.

He rose, shook out his blanket, and rolled comfortably in its warmth to let sleep come.

9

» » »

The two canoes slipped quietly downstream, only occasionally helped by a touch of the paddle in the hands of the steersmen. It was not advisable to go faster. The stream was narrow and winding, and there were rocks and sunken logs that could rip the belly out of the craft.

Many times this day, they had paused to get out of the canoes. The buckskins of all the men were wet to the knees from wading and pulling canoes over the shoals. Twice they had been forced to unload everything and portage around a waterfall or forbidding rapids.

Cartier was pleased that the marquis seemed conservative in his approach. Some would have foolishly taken chances in the unknown stream, but the judgment of this man seemed good. It was better, of course, to be overly cautious than to destroy one or both of the canoes with a poor guess.

The party arrived at the stream toward evening, and the voyageurs had launched one of the canoes to reconnoiter. They had returned with a good report. The stream seemed large enough to float the big war canoes, with a certain amount of care.

"Very well!" said the marquis crisply. "We stay here tonight, and start on tomorrow."

That, too, had been good judgment. It would have been foolhardy to start into unknown territory with the sun lowering. Best to camp here, a little early, and start fresh in the morning.

The native carriers were paid as agreed, with trade goods. They elected to spend the night and start back next day. Cartier took Small Bear aside.

"Do you know more of the country ahead?" he inquired.

"No. Very little. One river joins another."

"Do you speak the tongues of people downstream?"

"Some. Some not."

"Will they use sign talk?"

"Maybe so."

Cartier realized that, not knowing personally, the other would avoid a positive answer. Since he had not been there, Small Bear would refuse to say yes or no about anything.

"Maybe so," Cartier echoed. "But you know of no warlike tribes?"

"That is true, Woodchuck. You should watch carefully, though."

"Of course. My friend, we thank you for your help."

"It is nothing."

The two groups had parted next morning, and Cartier was to see the canoeing skills of the voyageurs demonstrated. Their clockwork precision was apparent as the canoes were launched and loaded. There seemed to be a place for everyone and everything. The division of responsibility was clear. The steersman, in the rear position, had ultimate authority over each craft. He could see all the other paddlers, and direct their efforts. Except, they did not need direction. The team moved like the well-oiled works of a clock, accomplishing what was needed.

When it became apparent that the stream was too tricky for full speed, the voyageurs laid down their paddles, except for the front man and the steersman in the rear. In this way they cautiously probed the winding course of the river. They had come little distance today, and Cartier was afraid that the marquis would be impatient. But it was not so.

"It goes well, Sergeant!" smiled the marquis as they pulled the canoes up on a sandbar and made camp for the night. "The stream begins to widen."

Cartier would not have noticed that. He was still frustrated by the constant pauses to unload, or wade and drag the canoes. However, it was true, he now realized. Late in the afternoon, they had passed the mouth of another good-sized stream. Since then, there had been fewer stops, more depth to the river. There were also small streams constantly joining the one on which they traveled. Yes, he could see, now that he studied the matter, that they were making much progress.

His eye fell on a sycamore across the river. The symmetry of its branches caught his attention. Yes, it was much like the river. Say a squirrel, for instance, started from the top and made its way downstream toward the trunk. Each fork that the creature passed would bring it to a larger bough, a more easily traversed pathway. Soon, it would be traveling on the larger limbs, then on the massive trunk itself. The tree is the trail for the squirrel, he thought, as the river is ours, and the trails on land are those for the deer and other animals.

Except for the buffalo. They needed no trails. The great herds moved with the seasons, migrating to areas of better graze as the greening of the prairie occurred.

He smiled to himself. He was thinking like the People, now. He remembered the Sun Dance and the celebration of the return of the grass and the buffalo. There was much that was good about the life he had shared with the People.

As they established the night camp, Cartier picked up his bow to make a circuit of the area. They would post night guards, and he wished to select the guard posts well before dusk.

The strip of timber where they camped, he discovered, was narrow. A well-traveled trail wound through it, probably used by deer. There was deer sign everywhere. He crossed the trail, marking in his mind a good spot for a sentry, and moved on toward the edge of the trees. There, stretching to the west, was open grassland. Not the wide skies and far horizons of the prairie, but grassland. It was like an invitation, a promise of the land farther west.

The setting sun colored the sky with pink and orange and purple, and he recalled an expression of the People: "Sun Boy chooses beautiful face-paint tonight."

There was a slight sound behind him, and he glanced around. A large buck deer stood, surprised at a whiff of unfamiliar scent. The creature was without antlers at this season, the furry knobs of new growth just starting to form.

Cartier was pleased. The startled demeanor of the animal was reassuring. It indicated that there was probably no other human presence in the area. His other reason for pleasure was more pragmatic. Fresh meat would be a welcome change from their dried supplies. They had been nearly a week on the journey. Quietly, he fitted an arrow to the string.

He had an advantage, as the buck was looking almost directly into the sun. He hoped that no unsuspected noise from the camp would startle the animal. Carefully, he drew the arrow to its head, and released the string.

There was no doubt, as the shaft flew, that it was on the mark. It was a feeling that he could not describe, but one that an experienced bowman knew. That arrow would strike true.

The buck lunged and leaped away, with the hunter in hot pursuit, fitting another arrow as he ran. The wounded animal was running wild, crashing irrationally into trees and brush in a frantic effort to escape the fatal thing deep in its vitals. It floundered and fell, to lie kicking in the last throes of death.

Cartier ran up, panting with exertion, and drew his

knife. A quick slash across the throat allowed the animal to bleed cleanly, and he waited a few moments, catching his breath while the struggles ceased.

He would call for help with the meat in a moment, but there was something he felt compelled to do. It was a private thing, a ritual. Deftly, he removed the head and lifted it to the crotch of a nearby tree. Turning back to the carcass, he slit the belly to expose the viscera. He sliced a thin strip of the warm liver and chewed it eagerly.

It was the first kill of the season. The depleted organ system of those limited to dry meat and pemmican for the winter cried out for the life-giving juices of fresh meat. The ritual bite of liver was half sacrament, half celebration of the season of greening.

There was one more thing. Cartier solemnly faced the deer's head in the tree and addressed it, bowing politely.

"We are sorry to kill you, my brother, but your flesh gives life to us. May your kind prosper and find green meadows."

It was an adaptation of the People's prayer to the buffalo, which had impressed the sergeant when intoned by Looks Far after the hunt. This was not the prairie, venison was certainly not in the same class with buffalo, but the idea was the same.

Cartier waited a moment, then turned to walk partway through the timber.

"Ho there," he called. "Someone help me with the meat."

10

Progress was much faster after the river widened. Cartier was somewhat puzzled. The size of the stream they traveled was that of the Big River, but he found no familiar landmarks. It had been several years, but there should have been something to remember, some sign that would reassure him.

To add to his confusion, the course of this river seemed slightly more southwest. It had seemed to him on the previous expedition that for the first days and weeks, even, they had traveled almost due south. Maybe even a bit southeast.

He squatted one morning, idly scratching lines in the sand, trying to clear his thinking. Now, if we started here, he pondered, his stick making an X at Fort Mishighan, and traveled due west, we came to the Big River. He sketched that stream into his crude map. But if we traveled *south*, as we did this time, we came to the headwaters of this stream. He drew another line, approximating the river they now traveled. Yes, the two were somewhat parallel. They must join somewhere below.

He tried to remember the few days before the accident. Had there not been a large river that emptied into the Big River? Yes, surely, from their left. It had not seemed important, because their mission had been pointed the other way, to the right of the river's course.

But now, he seemed to recall, there was some discussion at the time. The Big River had flowed nearly due east for several days, and Du Pres had seemed uneasy. It was not long after that, in the drizzle and fog. . . .

"Well, Sergeant, are we traveling properly?"

The marquis seemed cheerful as he squatted beside him.

"Yes, monsieur. At least, I think so."

"This is not the Big River?"

"Part of it, maybe. It looks different. I think we have not yet joined the main river."

"*Mon dieu!* Your Father of Rivers must be magnificent!"

"It is, monsieur. But I am not quite clear. See, here is Fort Mishi-ghan. We came this way."

He traced the marks in the sand with his stick.

"Now, we are about here, and the Big River is somewhere to the west."

"Yes. But they must join below here, no?"

"That is my thought, monsieur, but I do not know how far."

"What does it matter?" the other shrugged. "This is good traveling, and both branches go to the same river, do they not?"

"I suppose so, monsieur. There would be no other way."

It was later that night, and the moon was rising, when it became apparent that they were not alone. Cartier had had an uneasy feeling all evening, one that he could not quite define. He did not see or hear anything, it was more of an instinct. There was someone or something out there in the deepening dusk.

He recalled an odd print in the sand where they had paused for a noon stop. It had the appearance of the mark made by the prow of a canoe. He had seen it for only a moment as they beached the first canoe. Then the other craft pulled alongside, and the ripple of a wave washed against the sandbar. The mark he had noticed was gone.

He was uneasy enough to take special care in posting sentries, and to take the first watch himself. He had never objected to night watch, as some soldiers do. It was a time to be alone, to think, to enjoy the night sounds.

He found a vantage point, against the base of a large rock, and sank to a squatting position in its shadow. From here, he could see much of the skyline to the west of the river. Any intruder would come into his range of vision.

The sun had set, but its faint afterglow lingered while the creatures of the night came awake and began to speak. In the distance *Kookooskoos* sounded its hollow cry. Nearer at hand a night bird sounded its plaintive question, *"pour Pierre?"* Cartier had thought this bird amusing when he first heard its call, but there were those who thought otherwise. The ghostly sound in the night could easily conjure up visions of disembodied and lost souls.

From another angle came the cry of the night bird, questioning the whereabouts of the missing Pierre. It was answered from the timber to his right. These Pierre-birds, as he had come to think of them, were certainly numerous here.

Suddenly Cartier stiffened and became more alert. The birds were *too* numerous. Unless he was badly mistaken, some of the sounds he was hearing were made by human lips. He waited a moment, undecided. Then, cautiously, he puckered his lips and imitated the bird's call.

The result was startling. For a moment, nothing happened. Then, from a grassy hummock directly in front of him came an answering *"pour Pierre?"* The caller was not more than a stone's throw away.

Cartier waited, eyes riveted on the area of the hummock. A man rose and came straight toward him, crouching low as he moved. Cartier could see the warrior silhouetted against the sky. It was apparent that the other had interpreted the birdcall as originating with one of his

43

own party. And that, of course, meant that there were at least two, probably more, warriors out there in the darkness.

Cartier tensed his muscles to spring. The intruder came closer, paused, and seemed confused, sensing something wrong. He gave the *pour Pierre?* call again.

The man was too close for Cartier to answer the birdcall, yet not close enough to reach without giving advance warning. Cartier could have killed him easily and silently with the bow. At one time in his life he would have, without hesitation. Now he was reluctant, for reasons he would have found hard to explain. Besides, if he could capture the man alive, he might obtain information.

He laid his bow aside, as quietly as he could. He remained in his squatting position, so that he could see the other man's silhouette clearly. Neither man moved. It became a contest of who would take action first. Cartier was aware of the smell of the man. A faint suggestion of smoky cooking fires and native-tanned skins, sweat, and the grease with which face-paint was mixed. The People had insisted that with practice it was possible to tell to which tribe a person belonged by his scent. The subtle differences in food habits and methods of tanning caused the variation. Cartier wished for more experience. It might have been valuable now.

Probably not, though, he realized. He had little knowledge of tribes in this area anyway.

He was impatient. Something had to break the stalemate. He picked up a stick and tossed it quietly, beyond and to one side of the other man. The stick rattled against the woody stems of a clump of sumac, creating a satisfactory amount of noise as it bounced to the ground. The intruder whirled to face the sound, and instantly Cartier was upon him.

In another instant the sergeant was fighting for his life. The man was quick and wiry, much stronger than Cartier had expected. He was also armed with a knife, while

Cartier had sheathed his own weapon in the hope of capturing his foe alive.

They rolled over and over in a death struggle. Neither made a sound, beyond the coarse breathing of exertion. Cartier feared that the companions of the other would come to his assistance at any moment. He realized that the intruder would likewise wish to avoid rousing the camp.

It seemed a long time that they struggled. In reality, it was only a few minutes, but Cartier felt his strength ebbing. Most of all, he feared the slashing knife. He must avoid that at all costs.

He shifted his grip, using both hands on the wrist that wielded the weapon, bending the arm backward. If he could break the bone, his assailant would be disabled. Cartier was long past the goal of capturing the man. Now it was purely survival.

Just as it seemed the bone must snap, the knife dropped to the ground. The man gave a grunt of pain, and his straining muscles relaxed.

It might be a trick, Cartier realized, to put him off guard. But the knife was gone, the opponent disarmed. He paused a moment to catch his breath, holding pressure on the arm.

By moonlight, Cartier could see fear in the face of the other man. It appeared that he was hardly more than a boy. Possibly that explained the grunt of pain. Most warriors would have died in silence, and been proud to do so. His youth made this man no less dangerous, perhaps even more so. He was big and strong, and had accounted himself well.

Cartier was breathing somewhat more easily now. He shifted his weight slowly, rolling to sit astride the young man, placing a knee on the other's free arm. Now he freed his right hand, and began to use the sign talk.

"Listen!" he demanded. "I would talk with you."

The eyes of the captive grew large. He nodded. Cartier touched the knife at his belt.

"If you try to fight, I will kill you."

Again, the other nodded. Slowly, Cartier released his grip and relaxed, hand still at his knife.

"Now," he signed, "we talk."

11

» » »

"You know the sign talk?" the astonished warrior asked, in signs.

"Of course."

Cartier paused a moment. How should he begin?

"How are you called?" he asked finally.

"I am Pretty Weasel. And you?"

"Woodchuck."

"What is your tribe?"

"The Elk-dog People. Far to the west." Cartier pointed.

"But you come from the north."

"Yes. Listen! You are my captive. I will ask the questions."

The other man nodded.

"Now," began Cartier. "Where is your lodge?"

"Two sleeps." The man pointed downstream.

"On the river?"

"Yes."

"Why do you attack us?"

"We only watch. We do not know you. If you mean harm, we kill you."

It was the longest speech from the prisoner so far. The man was perfectly straightforward, it seemed. The actions he described were logical for those dwelling on the river.

But there was a potential problem. The party of the

47

marquis would have to pass the village of these warriors. The river dwellers would be experts in the art of making war in canoes, and would far outnumber the explorers.

His mind looked back in time again. Such things had been the responsibility of others, before. Brûle and Pale Star had negotiated with tribes they met. Now he, Woodchuck, carried this responsibility.

"Look." He signed for attention again. "We mean no harm."

He could see doubt in the face of the other man.

"We are only passing downriver. Then we will be gone."

There was little change in expression.

This was extremely important, Cartier realized. The village of this man, two sleeps away, was only the first they would encounter. Word of their coming would precede them. This first contact *must* be a good one. If it became unpleasant, the message filtering on down the river ahead of them would rouse the natives to war. It must not happen.

"My friend," Cartier signed, "we come in peace, but we are strong. My chief," he pointed to the camp, "has brought gifts for those who treat him well. For those who do not—" He touched the knife at his belt.

"What does he want?"

"Only safe passage. We will stop at your village two sleeps from now."

Pretty Weasel nodded.

"Now, go. Tell your chief."

The young man scrambled to his feet, still showing some doubt.

"I go, now?"

Cartier nodded.

Pretty Weasel hesitated a moment longer.

"Woodchuck," he signed. "I am made to think you speak truth. I will tell my chief."

"It is as I have said."

The young man turned and moved away, his figure

soon lost in the shifting shadows of the moonlight. Cartier heard the birdcall signal, and wondered if it was made by his recent prisoner.

It was some time later that the Bowman came to take the next watch.

"It is quiet, no?"

"Yes," answered Cartier. "There are men out there, but it should be quiet."

He showed the newcomer the concealed spot next to the rock, from which he could watch. He was glad that the sentry would be this man of experience. Somehow, the Bowman's whole demeanor spoke of competence. He was not quite certain of the others.

He started away, and then turned back. The sentry deserved to know the whole story.

"I have talked to one of them," he explained. "We will stop at their village two days downstream."

"*Mon dieu!*" the other said softly. "You have talked to them?"

Cartier nodded.

"But keep watch carefully anyway. I do not know these people."

The Bowman nodded agreement.

"Of course."

Cartier made his way back to the camp and rolled in his blanket. His muscles ached from the struggle, but he was so stimulated that he thought he would find sleep difficult. Despite his excitement, however, he was asleep almost instantly, with the sleep of exhaustion.

The camp was already stirring when he opened his eyes. The marquis was squatting beside him.

"Tell me, Sergeant, it is true you have talked to the natives?"

Word travels fast among soldiers, Cartier reflected with wry amusement. He sat up, wincing slightly as he used muscles so recently taxed to their limit.

"Yes, monsieur, I talked to one man."

"They are friendly, no?"

"To a point, yes. I told him we mean no harm, and will stop at their village. It is downstream, two days. I told him we have gifts for their chief."

"Is this wise?"

"Yes, monsieur. Word will then precede us, farther downstream. The tribes below will know of our coming, anyway. If we are known to be not dangerous, we will receive welcome rather than resistance."

"I see. This will not be considered a sign of weakness?"

"I think not, monsieur. We can make a show of strength when we approach. That is their way."

His mind wandered for a moment, back through the years. He and Sky-Eyes had been with the Eastern band of the People, when they approached the site of the annual Sun Dance. The mounted charge of young warriors in mock attack had been a hair-raising thing, but had been only a welcome to friends and relatives. He recalled the way they had been caught up in the excitement of the moment. They had loped their horses in reckless celebration, yelling and whooping with the rest.

An idea began to form in his mind. The voyageurs could put on quite a performance, one that would make a favorable impression on the residents of the village as they approached.

"We must make ourselves appear invincible, but generous," he explained to the marquis.

The nobleman nodded in agreement.

"It is much the same as diplomacy anywhere, no?" he smiled.

"Yes, monsieur, I suppose so. I have no experience in those matters."

"But you have! Already, you have negotiated with their envoy."

Cartier smiled to himself. There was no way in which he could explain to the marquis. The negotiation had come about almost accidently, at knife point, after a struggle that could easily have ended in death.

In a sense, he supposed, that was diplomacy.

12

» » »

Cartier found his skills of observation returning. He remembered the morning they had stood on the hill overlooking the River of Swans. Pale Star had pointed out subtle differences. The white mists of morning hung over the river, but at one point in the distance the appearance was different. The layers of mist appeared blue-gray, and rose vertically above the blanket of white. That, Star had pointed out, marked the location of the village they sought. The warm smoke from the cooking fires caused this appearance.

It was so this morning. He turned and called to the marquis.

"Monsieur! There is the village!"

He pointed in a general direction. The area involved was hidden behind the twists and turns of the river, but above the trees rose a smudge of bluish smoke.

Almost at the same moment, a canoe swept around the bend ahead. It was one of the big war canoes, with several men manning paddles. The craft was closely followed by two more. All of the strangers were heavily armed and their faces painted.

For a moment, Cartier was afraid they had been betrayed. Their party was badly outnumbered, and at a disadvantage in a fight. At any rate, it was time to put their plan into motion. He called to the marquis.

"Now, monsieur!"

"Bring the canoes into line," the marquis barked.

The second canoe swung forward, abreast of the other, and the musketeers made ready. The natives were closer now, shouting and brandishing weapons. The hair rose on the back of Cartier's neck. They were scarcely a bowshot away. It was difficult to remember that this was only a mock attack. If, indeed, it was not about to become the real thing.

"Ready?" he called, glancing at the other canoe.

The grim faces of the voyageurs reflected a certain anxiety, but confidence.

"Remember, it is just a show. No one is to be hurt."

The two parties drew closer, and Cartier thought that it was time for their surprise move.

"Now!" he commanded.

The double crack of two muskets resounded across the river, rattled against the timber ahead, and boomed again in the distance in an echo off the far hillsides. White smoke hung in a cloud over the water. The voyageurs set up a cheer.

There was a moment of shocked silence from the other canoes, and then frantic motion. The natives maneuvered skillfully, whipping the canoes around to retreat.

"Again!" shouted Cartier.

Two more muskets boomed skyward, while the first pair were reloaded. The retreat accelerated, and the voyageurs cheered again.

"That is enough," called Cartier. "We must let them save face."

The musketeers calmly reloaded their weapons, and the canoes were allowed to drift downstream toward the village. An occasional touch of the paddle by the steersmen kept them pointed with the current.

It was some time before they rounded one of the endless bends of the river and saw a long stretch of water with a cluster of log houses at the other end. Now a few canoes were skirting cautiously near the banks, careful to keep a safe distance.

Cartier, in the prow of one canoe, raised his right arm, palm forward, in the universal sign. The absence of a weapon signified "I am unarmed, I come in peace." Some of the canoes came closer now, perhaps encouraged by this sign. A man in one of the vessels waved in greeting. Cartier recognized Pretty Weasel, his erstwhile prisoner.

"Greetings, Weasel," he signed. "It is well with you?"

The canoe approached, its occupants a trifle nervous. The vessel swung about to travel with those of the voyageurs, and others joined the growing fleet.

"Welcome, Woodchuck," Pretty Weasel signed with a grin. "Yes, it is well. It is as you said? No fighting? Gifts for our chief?"

"No fighting. We come in peace."

"It is good."

They were approaching the shore near the village now, and maneuvered to bring the canoes to the bank.

"Should we show them another volley?" asked the marquis.

"I think not, monsieur. It goes well already. That might alarm them."

They beached the canoes and stepped ashore, still wary and on the lookout for any treachery. The natives hung back, equally ill at ease. Pretty Weasel strode forward, right hand raised. Slightly behind and to each side followed two more warriors.

"Welcome!" Pretty Weasel signed. "This is your chief?"

"Yes," nodded Cartier. "He is a great chief." He turned to the marquis. "Monsieur, this is the man I told you of."

The marquis held up a hand in greeting.

"Come," motioned Weasel. "I will take you to our chief."

He turned and led the way among the log houses toward a larger one. Cartier remembered that these river tribes sometimes had a "longhouse," or council lodge.

"Here," Pretty Weasel pointed.

The marquis bent to follow their guide into the lodge, with Cartier close behind. The voyageurs had remained with the canoes.

The chief was seated at the far end of the room, flanked by several whom Cartier presumed to be subchiefs. Pretty Weasel stepped forward to speak to the chief. The old man nodded and spoke in sign talk.

"Welcome to my lodge. What do you want here?"

"Nothing, my chief. We are only passing on the river. Then we will be gone. This is our chief, who has gifts for you."

"He does not know the hand signs?"

"No. He is new to this area. His lodge is far away."

The old chief seemed satisfied, and the marquis motioned for Cartier to open the pack they had brought. Cartier had helped to choose the contents the night before. Some bright beads and metal ornaments, mirrors, and a small knife for the chief. The gifts were quickly distributed.

"Now," the chief signed, "a feast is being prepared. But there is one other thing."

He paused, and spoke quickly to Pretty Weasel. The young man smiled and nodded, then turned to Cartier.

"He wants to see you make the thunder-sticks boom," he stated. "How do you do that?"

13

» » »

The entire population of the village turned out for the demonstration. They lined up along the shore or found observation points among trees and rocks. It was a carnival atmosphere as Cartier and the marquis planned the scenario.

The musketeers would stand on the bank and shoot at an object in the river. That way, even a near miss would throw up a splash of water. A canoe was launched to tow a driftwood log upstream and release it.

When all was ready, Pretty Weasel, in the canoe, out of sight behind the trees, gave a shout. The canoe skirted rapidly along the shore, to arrive before the floating target. The paddlers had barely time to reach the village when the log came into view. It bobbed majestically along in the current, presenting a good target.

It was almost exactly opposite the crowd when the marquis gave the command.

"Une, deux, trois!"

Four muskets roared as one, and splinters of wood sprayed into the air. There were exclamations of astonishment and fear, and some of the more timid of the tribe fled for their lives.

Pretty Weasel drove his canoe forward to retrieve the

log target. There was a brief struggle until they could pull the unwieldy object out of the tow of the current. Then, in the backwater near the shore, they were able to drag it back for inspection.

Excitement increased as the log was dragged up the bank, and the observers could actually touch the damaged surface and put fingertips in the holes made by the heavy lead balls.

"This is very strong medicine, Woodchuck," signed Weasel seriously. "Worm-Face must be a great chief."

"Worm-Face?"

"Yes, he wears the worms on his lip."

The marquis, who had been watching the hand signs, interrupted.

"Cartier, I am understanding only a little of this sign talk. What is he saying?"

The sergeant was at a loss for a moment. How could he diplomatically translate the fact that these people had chosen such a name for the young nobleman?

"Monsieur, they say yours is strong medicine. You are a great chief, who commands the warriors with thunder-sticks."

"Yes, yes," the marquis responded impatiently. "But there was the sign for 'he is called.' What did he say?"

Cartier took a deep breath.

"Well, you know that they choose a name for people. It usually describes physical appearance or an event. I am called 'Woodchuck.'"

"Yes, I remember. So, I am Chief Thunder-Sticks?"

"No, monsieur, not exactly."

He was in an uncomfortable spot. He must try to explain that the names bestowed by these people did not carry any stigma. They were only descriptive. The most memorable thing about the appearance of the marquis was, to these people, his moustache. They had never before seen anyone clean-shaven but with a trimmed and waxed moustache. Therefore, the name they gave the marquis reflected this observation.

Cartier had found it mildly amusing, but the situation had now become very delicate. If the marquis became angry over the name, there could be serious results.

"Monsieur," Cartier began cautiously, "they will name the voyageurs the 'thunder-stick men' or some such thing. You, of course, are their chief. But the thing they see as different in your appearance is your moustache."

"The moustache?"

"Yes, monsieur."

The marquis thought a moment.

"Then, I am called 'Moustache'?"

"Yes, something like that," Cartier mumbled.

The marquis was a quick thinker, however.

"Sergeant, you said a moustache is unfamiliar to them. They have never seen one."

"Yes, that is right."

"Then, they have no word for it," the marquis observed.

Cartier had not foreseen this line of conversation. He stood, hesitating.

"So, what word do they use?"

The sergeant took a deep breath. He could not evade any longer.

"Worms, monsieur."

"Mon dieu! Worms?"

"Yes, monsieur. They think the appearance is that of worms on the face."

There was a moment of shocked surprise. Cartier fearfully waited for the marquis to explode into anger. Perhaps he had made a mistake in revealing so much to the nobleman. But no, he would find out, sometime, and might be more angered at any deception. No, it was better to get it out, now, to weather the anger, and put it behind them.

The marquis still stood staring, his mouth open in unbelief. He raised a hand to touch the carefully trimmed moustache. It did, Cartier observed, resemble a pair of caterpillars, poised head to head, with the waxed tips extending like the creatures' horns. But a nobleman was not likely to appreciate that. Cartier waited for the explosion of rage.

Suddenly the marquis threw his head back and howled with laughter.

"Worms!" he yelled in delight. "Worms-on-the-Face!"

Cartier nodded, still uneasy.

"Actually not worms, Sergeant," the other corrected more calmly. "Worms are smooth, while the moustache is hairy. Caterpillars, more likely."

He chuckled again.

"Yes, monsieur. My translation may be at fault," Cartier apologized, still uncomfortable.

"It is no matter. Look, this means they have accepted me, no?"

"Yes, perhaps so."

"Then, it is a good thing. Worms!"

Cartier gave vent to a heartfelt sigh of relief. It appeared that the marquis would actually be proud of his new title.

Arrangements were progressing for the feast in honor of the visitors. The voyageurs, except for those guarding the canoes, were mingling freely with the natives. Dusky beauties cast coquettish glances at appreciative Frenchmen, and a few began to pair off for the evening.

Cartier had not really considered, before. The customs of these tribes were considerably different from those of the People. Especially regarding women, it seemed. These girls seemed to have an uninhibited, open sexuality. That would not have been tolerated by the stricter code of his wife's tribe.

He was convinced of this when a man approached to offer Cartier his wife for the night. Such a thing would be shockingly immoral among the People. He declined gracefully, and then was amused at himself for doing so. At one time he would have been eager to accept the favor. Odd, he recalled, that he found himself willing to follow the ethics of the tribe who had accepted him as

one of their own. He was more amused than disturbed.
Perhaps, as he found himself again among the tribes, it
was natural for him to fall into their ways again.

He thought back to his first encounter with Pretty
Weasel. He had identified himself, not as *Fran-coy*, but as
a man of the Elk-dog People. Why had he done such a
thing?

His thoughts were interrupted by Pretty Weasel.

"Come, Woodchuck! The feast is ready!"

14
» » »

The canoes were loading to depart, now. Sleepy-looking voyageurs, exhausted from a night of revelry, were readying the craft for the day's journey.

Cartier was taking leave of Pretty Weasel, in sign talk.

"You have helped us much, my friend. We will remember your people with happiness."

"And you, also."

Cartier looked around. The canoes were not quite ready.

"Tell me, Weasel, of the river below here. It is good traveling?"

"Yes. Many turns. Like a snake."

He made a snakelike motion with his hand.

"But it runs into the Big River?"

"The *Missi-sepe*, Father of Water? No, Woodchuck. Into the *O-hay-oh*. That joins the *Missi-sepe*, but far below. I have never been that far."

Cartier experienced a moment of panic. He was not in the area he had thought.

"Then what is this river?"

He had been thinking of this as one of the headwaters of the Big River, perhaps the one known to natives near the fort as the *Ille-nois*.

"This is called the *Ouabache* by my people. You thought it somewhere else?"

Weasel showed his concern.

"No, it is no matter."

It really is not, he reminded himself. We go to the Big River's mouth. How we get there is not important.

At least, he thought not. It was purely an exploring trip. The marquis only sought a way to the southern sea. This would provide that way, and a direct one.

Why, then, should he be concerned? He had not realized that he was looking forward to reliving the previous days on the river, even the area of the accident. That must have been, he had learned later, at the mouth of the *Peki-tanoui*, the "Muddy," as it was called by tribes in the area. It was confusing, since different tribes used their own names for geographic features. He had heard tribes farther to the west refer to the same stream as the *Emissourita*, where it was joined by the *Canseh*.

When he tried to imagine the land as a map, in his mind, he became completely confused. The river they now traveled would eventually take them into the Big River, the *Missi-sepe*, but not by the way he had thought. It would be "far" to the south, Weasel said. It seemed that at no time would they ever be traveling a portion of the river that Cartier had ever seen before. It was an embarrassing thought, that he was the party's guide, but he might as well have been lost.

He had to admit, though, if he was honest with himself, that this was not the problem. He had counted heavily on seeing familiar places again, and now there would be none. That, in truth, was his disappointment.

His reverie was interrupted by the approach of the marquis.

"Sergeant, you have expressed our thanks to—'Weasel,' is it?"

"Yes, monsieur. And he tells me the chief will be out to see us off. We will thank him then."

The marquis nodded.

61

"I hope the chief will hurry. I want to make good time today."

"Yes, they will know this. It is custom to come at the last moment. A matter of dignity."

The marquis chuckled.

"More diplomacy, no?"

"Perhaps."

"Very well, we wait. Sergeant, would it not be helpful to have this Weasel go with us as interpreter? He seems to communicate well."

Cartier started to protest that he could handle communication himself. He was a little resentful at the suggestion. Before he could answer, however, an idea occurred to him. It would be of great help to have someone familiar with the culture of the tribes along the river. Pretty Weasel could speak their tongues. In addition, he was familiar with the rivers and their courses.

"An excellent thought, monsieur! Shall I ask him?"

"Yes, by all means!"

Cartier turned and signed to the young man.

"My chief asks if you will go with us."

"With you?"

Pretty Weasel seemed suspicious.

"Yes, to speak the tongues of tribes on the river. To guide us. It would please me, too."

A broad smile now creased the face of the young man.

"Tell Worm-Face I will come. I go now to get my pack and tell my parents."

Cartier had already gathered that Weasel was unmarried, and lived with his parents. The young warrior hurried away.

"He will come with us?" inquired the marquis.

"Yes. I think he is pleased. This will be good, monsieur. He knows the river and I do not."

The marquis nodded.

"You said you have never been on this portion, Sergeant?"

Cartier paused a moment. It would be best to be truthful, he thought.

"Monsieur, from what Pretty Weasel tells me, we will not travel any river that I do know."

"We are on the wrong course?"

"No, no, monsieur. The waters all join downstream, flow into the Big River, what they call the *Missi-sepe*. This one joins it farther south than I thought."

"I see. But it goes to the sea? The Gulf?"

"Yes, monsieur."

Pretty Weasel had returned, carrying his rawhide pack. Cartier knew that it had been hastily crammed with dried meat and other supplies, of whatever sort might be used by these river tribes. Fish, perhaps, and possibly corn.

"Tell him Worm-Face is pleased to have him join us," the marquis instructed.

Cartier did so. Weasel nodded respectfully and signed directly to the marquis.

"It is good, my chief."

"Put your pack in that canoe," the marquis pointed.

He appeared pleased to use the rudiments of sign talk.

The village chief now approached, flanked by his sub-chiefs, for the ceremonial farewell. He seemed impressed that one of his young warriors would accompany the party.

There were sign talk exchanges, promises of everlasting friendship, and wishes for a good journey.

Cartier happened to remember an object in the buckskin pouch at his waist. He had wished to give something to Pretty Weasel before he left, and had spent many spare moments on a carving. It represented an eagle's head, whittled from a carefully chosen crooked stick. He had realized the pleasure, almost a reverence, that his whittled objects inspired among the tribes farther west.

Now, with Weasel traveling with them, he could make something later. This medicine-stick he would present to the chief.

"With our thanks, my chief," he signed as he handed the object ceremonially.

Cartier could see immediately that his gift had hit the mark, as the chief's face glowed with pleasure.

He could not foresee that, years later, another exploring expedition would be shown an eagle-shaped medicine-stick by an ancient chieftain. The chief would boast that it was a gift, made and presented by his good friend, Chief Woodchuck, of whom they had never heard.

15

» » »

"Like a snake!" Cartier exclaimed in frustration, accompanying his remark with the appropriate sign.

Pretty Weasel chuckled and nodded. For days they had traveled a series of loops and bends of the river. At any given moment they might be traveling any direction by the compass. Not only south or west, but due east, even northeast at times, as the river twisted to follow the terrain.

It was extremely frustrating to Cartier not to know his basic direction. The sun's arc helped somewhat, but after the meandering of the river, the constant change in direction, it was good to reorient by the stars. They would camp for the night, and after the fall of darkness, he would locate the Seven Hunters, and from that, their lodge at the Real-star. The Real-star brought a sense of direction, of permanence. Cartier wondered if it moved at all, or if it had hung there in the north since time began, with all the others wheeling around it every night.

Sometimes, on this confusing river journey, the Real-star was not at all where he expected. But it was always there.

"Does the river run straighter below?" he asked.

"Maybe," Weasel answered honestly. "I have never been to the *Missi-sepe*."

"I know. It is like a snake as far as you have been?"

"Yes."

Weasel was silent a moment and then signed again.

"There is a town, two sleeps from here, where we should stop."

"They are your people?"

"Yes. Same people, different town. They will welcome us."

"Good. I will tell Worm-Face."

"It is just over those hills."

"But you said two sleeps."

"By the river. One sleep over the hills."

Weasel bent and drew an arc in the sand, shaped like a long horseshoe.

"Here are we. Here, the town. Around the river, two sleeps."

He held up two fingers. Then he made a short stroke across the narrow neck of the loop.

"Across, one day's travel."

"Could we carry canoes?"

"I think not, Woodchuck. It is easier by river."

Cartier was tempted to argue. Anything to end the frustration of twisting and turning, traveling around three days to gain two days' distance. Had they not gone overland before?

Yes, he realized, but they had hired carriers to help with the supplies and baggage.

"I could go and tell them we are coming," Weasel offered.

Cartier thought about that for a moment. The idea was a good one.

"And I could go with you."

It was a chance at a pleasant diversion. He could escape from the tedium of the river, and travel with this pleasant young man who had become his friend. It was difficult to realize now that not many days ago Pretty Weasel

66

had tried his utmost to kill him. Now, Cartier would trust him with his life.

"Weasel, will they have any trouble on the river?"

Weasel smiled and shrugged.

"The river only flows downstream."

"I will speak to our chief."

He rose and walked over to where the marquis relaxed on his blanket.

"Monsieur, Weasel says there is a town, two sleeps downriver. They are of his tribe, and it would be well to stop there for the night."

The marquis nodded.

"Why not? We could use a little diversion."

"Then, monsieur, perhaps it would be well if Weasel and I go ahead to tell them we are coming?"

"Go ahead? How do you propose to do that, Sergeant?"

"Weasel says the distance is short overland, because of a long bend in the river. The town is that way, across the hills."

"*Mon dieu!* Another loop? Well, go ahead!"

"Yes, monsieur. We will leave in the morning."

He hurried back to share the plan with Weasel, who seemed pleased. They fed their little campfire and prepared to retire.

"Woodchuck, have you ever had a wife?" the other man asked unexpectedly in sign talk.

Odd, Cartier reflected. Since he left the People, he had never once mentioned his marriage to anyone.

"Yes. I married a woman of the Elk-dog People, and became one of them. I have a son. He would be five, six summers now."

"Where is your wife?"

"Dead. She was killed when my son was small. That is when I left to return to Mishi-ghan. I am really *Francoy*."

"Yes, I know. You have not seen your son since then?"

"No."

"My heart is sad for you, Woodchuck."

Cartier was embarrassed by the sympathy of the other, yet he appreciated the gesture. He remembered one of the men with whom he had hunted buffalo.

"My food tastes like ashes in my mouth," the hunter had said during the mourning period for Pink Cloud.

Yes, it was good to have someone to share grief. He had had no one. He had tried to make his hurt go away by forgetting, denying that it had happened at all, and returning to his soldier's duties.

He had been unsuccessful, he now realized. The hurt was as bad as before. But he had forgotten the sympathy of the People, how they had attempted to console him in his grief. He had been unable to accept it at the time, in the throes of his bereavement. Now, he was able to share his tragedy with a sympathetic friend, and benefit from it. Could it be possible that he was making progress?

The custom of the People was to mourn for three days, to sing the Song of Mourning, to end the grief by recognizing it. He wished that he had understood better at the time. He had refused the support and assistance of friends. He wondered if he had seemed unappreciative.

"Thank you, my friend," he signed to Weasel.

He rolled in his blanket and turned his back to the fire. He wished that he could thank his friends and the relatives of Pink Cloud, who had tried to help him.

But they were far away to the west, beyond the River of Swans.

16

》》》

Their stopover at the village of Pretty Weasel's people proved a replica of the previous stop. The major difference was that this village had more time to prepare.

Weasel had explained the situation in detail on the evening of their arrival, and a welcome was made ready. Despite the advance explanations about the noise and smoke of the muskets, there were those who panicked and ran. Most were merely fascinated.

Weasel had relatives to visit, and Cartier took advantage of the visit to inquire about the river beyond this point.

"Ask your uncle all about the river," Cartier suggested.

Weasel nodded, pleased at the prospect of an important place in the planning of the journey. He spent a long time in conversation and then turned again to Cartier.

"He says the junction of the river is a few sleeps. Maybe three or four. He does not know whether we travel fast or slow."

"This will be the Big River, the *Missi-sepe?*"

"No, no. We are still on the *Ouabache*. We will reach the *O-hay-oh* first."

"Ask him about the *Missi-sepe.*"

Weasel turned and conversed for a little while with his kinsman, then turned back.

"He does not know. The Big River is somewhere beyond."

"A long way?"

"I think not. A few sleeps."

He turned to verify this impression.

"Yes, that is right. A few sleeps to the *O-hay-oh*, a few more to the *Missi-sepe*."

Cartier was pleased, when they moved on, to feel that at least he knew what to expect.

If he expected that the river would stop the snakelike course after it joined the *O-hay-oh*, he was badly disappointed. The gyrations only became worse.

He had learned to evaluate direction and distance as the plains tribes did, by distant landmarks. It was extremely frustrating for him to pick a distant hill in the morning to guide by. It was on all sides through the day, front, right, left, even behind them, and next morning it would still be there. It seemed that they would never pass and leave it behind. He had a good idea of the distance of various landmarks, and how long it would have taken on a good buffalo horse.

But they were not traveling even a moderately straight line, and the canoes, though good for river travel, were far from comparing with a horse. Cartier had thrilled to the use of his horse. He had ridden his best horse when he left the People. He traded it to a man of one of the river tribes for a canoe in which to continue his tragic journey upriver back to civilization. Horses were not yet in general use in New France.

It was no matter, now. They were committed to this trip on the river. It was easy, pleasant traveling, and Cartier was a little puzzled that he was so bored and frustrated. That was basically foreign to his easygoing nature. But the old memories kept crowding back, reminding him of the happiness of his year on the prairie.

Yes, that must be it, the knowledge that out there, beyond the forested hills and the meandering river, were the big sky and the far horizons of the prairie.

Their first sight of the Big River, the *Missi-sepe*, Father of Rivers, was a thrilling moment. A fisherman they had encountered the day before had told Weasel that they were close to the junction of the rivers.

"One sleep." He held up an index finger.

The information had been accurate. They could tell that they were traveling now through a flat, low-lying flood plain. Then they rounded a fringe of willows and the breadth of the Big River stretched before them.

The voyageurs in the lead canoe set up a cheer, followed by the others. The face of the marquis was flushed with excitement.

"The River!" he chortled. "Cartier, you have done it! You have brought us to the River."

Embarrassed, Cartier smiled and said nothing. How could he take credit for this successful phase of the expedition, knowing as he did that it had been pure dumb luck? He had even put them on the wrong river to begin with. His heart was heavy.

"We stop early!" shouted the marquis. "Cartier! Which bank?"

"West," called Cartier, for no good reason.

He would have attempted to explain, if necessary, that the current of the smaller river would probably sweep across the main river and lose its strength, to deposit a flat, sandy bar somewhere a short distance below. He wasn't certain of this, but he seemed to remember it from somewhere, and it seemed reasonable. He hated to admit, even to himself, that it was mostly a yearning to set foot once more on land west of the Big River.

They swept across, pausing to notice the different color of the two rivers. They seemed to run side by side for a time before mixing, to lose their identity in one muddy sameness.

They beached the canoes on the convenient sandbar

71

that Cartier had hoped to find, and sprang ashore to make camp.

"Careful," called Cartier. "We don't know this area."

It was only a habit. There were no signs of human habitation at this point. Nevertheless, he determined to make sure that they were not taken by surprise. They would post guards with special care.

"Cartier! Could you find fresh meat?" the marquis called.

"We will try."

He motioned to Pretty Weasel and picked up his bow. They should explore the area, anyway, and find places to post sentries.

"There is a good spot," pointed Weasel.

Cartier nodded.

"Good. I will take the first watch. You change with me later. We will put one of the others over there."

They moved back through the timber, looking carefully for traces of deer or elk. Finally Weasel pointed.

"You go that way, I go this."

They separated and continued the hunt. It seemed only a few moments before there was a crashing in the underbrush, and a shout from Weasel. Cartier hurried in the direction of the sound.

Pretty Weasel was standing over a fat yearling buck, the spike antlers fuzzy with summer's velvet. He smiled happily.

"We have meat!" he signed.

He drew his knife to begin skinning.

17

» » »

Darkness had fallen, and Cartier squatted comfortably at his sentry post. Everyone had eaten well, and he could hear some of the voyageurs, not yet ready to retire after the day's accomplishment, singing songs of home and girls left behind.

The night was warm and damp, the smells of the river powerful in his nose. He was trying to reorient himself to the land.

At this point, the Big River seemed to flow a trifle east of south, but that was no matter. His directions were sure. He had seen Sun Boy drop below earth's rim in the distance. True, earth's rim was obscured by trees and hills, but he knew it was there.

He calculated that they must be farther south than he had ever been, to judge from the size of the river. It was much wider than he had expected. The air was also hot and heavy, the mosquitoes clinging and lazy. He was glad his buckskins were well smoked. At least, everything but face and hands was protected. He had rubbed venison fat on those areas. It was fortunate that the river seemed to cool the south breeze a little as it stirred the leaves of the trees around him. Otherwise it could have been quite intolerable.

He listened to the night sounds in the distance. There was the Pierre-bird, and another that he did not recognize. The soft call of *Kookooskoos* floated in ghostly cadence on the night breeze.

It was good, thought Cartier. Everything as it should be. And, just a few sleeps in the direction Sun Boy had taken, maybe a trifle farther north, would be the People. He found himself straining his eyes to see as far to the west as possible. Ridiculous, he told himself. What could you see? You only wish your spirit to reach out because your son is out there.

"Mon dieu," he muttered, half aloud. "What a strange thought!"

It was like something Looks Far would say, this talk of spirits reaching out.

"Woodchuck?" a quiet voice spoke in the tongue of the People.

Cartier jumped, startled. Then he remembered. He had taught Weasel the word for his name in that language.

"Weasel? You are early."

He pointed at the Seven Hunters.

"Yes. I did not know the songs."

Cartier nodded, understanding.

"I have been talking with Worm-Face. He used the sign talk well."

Was Weasel trying to tell him something? They had already noticed this. It was also true that Pretty Weasel, naturally adept at language, was rapidly learning French. Cartier could see that the young man had the potential to become a valuable interpreter. So, why had he come out here to the guard post?

Well, it was time to play the waiting game. Weasel would proceed when he was ready. There was a long time of silence, broken by a slap at a mosquito.

"They bite hard tonight," observed Cartier.

"Yes. I brought your blanket."

He handed the blanket, and Cartier drew it around his neck and head, protecting against the biting creatures.

"Good. Thank you."

"I have brought your pack, too."

"My pack?"

"Yes."

Weasel indicated the shapeless form on the ground.

"I have put some meat in it, a few beads."

"But, Weasel, what—?"

"I am made to feel that you should find your son."

"But—"

Weasel held up his hand.

"I will tell Worm-Face that I saw you, took over guard watch, and you started back to camp. I did not see you again."

Cartier sputtered in consternation.

"Woodchuck, you have been good to me. You spared my life, when most would have killed me. Now, I help you. Go home!"

The strange, unearthly thing about all this, Cartier realized numbly, is that it seems to make sense. Here is Weasel, whom I have known only a short while, encouraging me to desert my post, promising to cover for me, and the whole thing seems logical.

Actually, he would not be putting the expedition in any danger. Weasel would be a better scout, anyway. He was relating well to the marquis, and had already proved valuable to the party.

Cartier could go to see about his son, then make his way back to civilization. He could later say that he had heard something suspicious, gone to investigate, and become lost in the darkness. He could think of something later. Maybe Du Pres would come back with him, if he could find him.

Weasel picked up the pack and held it out to him.

"Here, Woodchuck. Go home. It is right."

Hardly realizing what he was doing, Cartier shrugged his shoulders into the straps. Then he fumbled in his pouch, to draw out the carving he had been making. He pressed it into Weasel's hand.

"Here, my friend. My medicine gift to you. Now, I go home."

He glanced at the Seven Hunters and the Real-star, and started northwest with long strides. He did not pause until he reached the low crest of the ridge. Then he looked back.

In the distance by the river, he could see the twinkling lights of the campfires. He paused only a moment, then swung along a dimly lit trail.

Somewhere in the dark, a night bird cried its plaintive question.

"Where's Pierre?"

18

» » »

The journey across country was a worrisome one for Cartier. In later times, he found that he had almost no memory for it.

He was constantly beset by doubts and conflicting emotions. On one hand, he was depressed by the enormity of the wrong he had done in abandoning his duty. On the other, he was relieved to be righting another wrong, the abandoning of his son. There were times, when traveling was good and he thought of the prairie to the west, that all seemed right with the world. He would stand tall and strong on the crest of a ridge with the breeze filling his lungs, and exult in all of creation. He felt strong, capable, efficient, and above all, *right*.

Then, in the dark of night, or on a day when lowering clouds pressed down on the world, he would have doubts. He would become morose over his desertion of duty, and stare at his campfire for hours. At these times, he felt weak and ineffective and small.

There was the entire problem of right and wrong, of conflicting duties that could not both be respected. Just when it seemed he could no longer survive the emotions and doubts that threatened his sanity, he would be forced to forget all the worrisome thoughts. Relief, as it seemed, from the mental anguish, came in the form of physical danger.

He was lost in thought, his awareness far away, when he nearly stepped on the real-snake. The creature was sunning itself in the middle of the game trail Cartier was following. Only the warning buzz of its rattles prevented his injury. He stopped in his tracks, his knife drawn almost by reflex and poised to throw downward. At the same time he froze, motionless. Any movement might cause the snake to strike.

The creature lay in a loose coil, taking advantage of the sun's rays. Its pastime had been interrupted by an intruder, and the real-snake now had assumed a position of defense and resentment. The neck and upper body were drawn into a tight s curve. Like the wanderings of the cursed river, Cartier observed, and then wondered at himself for such an illogical thought in this moment of crisis. The distal finger of the tail stood precisely upright, vibrating faster than the eye could see.

He had been told long ago that the sound of the real-snake's rattle, once heard, can never be forgotten. It is true, he thought, a sound one can never forget.

The snake, too, was frozen motionless except for the vibrating tail. Its head pointed directly toward his left foot. It was a strange face-off. Cartier could have struck downward with the thrown knife. It should be an easy throw, but suppose, just suppose, he missed. He would be completely unprotected, without fumbling the ax out of his belt, or preparing to fit an arrow to his bowstring. That would take far too long. There would not even be time to jerk back his foot, so lightning-fast would be the snake's strike.

Yet, the snake had *not* struck. At least, not yet. Sweat trickled down the back of Cartier's neck and between his shoulder blades inside his buckskin shirt. His palms became clammy, and he could feel his heart racing. He wondered for a moment if the real-snake could hear the frantic pounding.

Still, nothing happened. He began to think of the approach of the People to a situation of this sort. He realized he was reverting more and more to their ways as he came nearer their country.

The People would not hesitate for a moment to kill a real-snake, if it became a threat. He had seen it done, when one of the creatures was discovered in the middle of the meadow where the horse herd was at night pasture. Yet, an entire hunting party had once detoured around a hillock where a large real-snake sunned, leaving the creature unharmed.

Perhaps it was a taboo like that of the bears. The People never hunted bear, and would never eat bear meat, but it was permissible to kill one in self-defense, he had been told. It was much the same with the real-snake, he supposed. If the snake represented a risk, there was no taboo in self-defense.

Certainly, there was risk here, but as the heartbeats ticked past, it did not seem to be increasing. He took a deep breath and slowly exhaled.

"Little Brother," he said softly, "I am sorry to have disturbed your lodge. Let us go our way in peace."

The sharp vibration of the rattles slowed to a tentative rustle, like that of dry leaves in the breeze of autumn, and then stopped. Slowly, the tight muscles of the snake's head and neck seemed to soften and relax. The coils of the body, thick as Cartier's wrist, seemed to dissolve in fluid motion. The snake moved toward the shelter of a jumbled pile of rocks and brush.

It was unprotected now, and he could easily kill it without danger to himself. At one time he would have done so. Perhaps, even, a few weeks ago. But, somehow, he felt himself changing. Unless it served some useful purpose, why end the creature's life?

Perhaps it was like sparing the life of Pretty Weasel. More accurately, the other side of the coin. That had been for a specific purpose, the gathering of information. If one had a purpose, it would make a difference. The

People, he recalled, would hunt and kill dozens or hundreds of buffalo, but made use of them for food, lodge covers, robes, clothing, tools, and ornaments. Still, there was the ceremony over the first kill of the season, the apology for the taking of life.

And the People gloried in their songs of war. They had had little conflict in a generation, but the songs and dances told of glorious victories of the past, and the killing of hundreds of the enemy.

The snake had disappeared, now. The entire episode seemed unreal. Had his words actually reassured the creature, and made it do as he wished? Probably not, he decided. It undoubtedly was just ready to stop its posturing and retreat at that moment. Nevertheless . . .

"Thank you, Little Brother," he called after the real-snake.

Then, immediately, he felt very foolish. He sheathed his knife and moved on, now a bit more cautious where he stepped.

He wondered considerably about the experience. For a moment, there, he had felt that he knew the thoughts of the snake, had been "inside its head," as the People would say. Was this the way it would be on a vision quest? Maybe, he thought as he traveled on, it would be good to go on a vision quest. He would ask Looks Far about it. Or Red Feather, his wife's father. Yes, he would inquire.

He stopped for the night, and watched Sun Boy paint himself and go to his lodge on the other side. The stars began to appear, and he watched a long time before rolling in his blanket to sleep. His dream that night was of a council, where he appeared before the chief of all the real-snakes to negotiate for safe passage through their country.

19
» » »

Cartier was not sure of his direction. He was merely
heading northwest, knowing that he must eventually
come to the area frequented by the People. He believed
he would know the River of Swans if he encountered it.
But, its appearance might not be the same if he approached it at another point, farther downstream.

Well, no matter. When he felt near enough, he would
ask. Growers, he had learned during his year on the prairie, could be depended upon for information. They
traded with all comers, so their neutrality was assured.
Their information was also up-to-date, since they gathered the latest news and gossip along with the meat and
robes traded by the hunting tribes.

But if he was unsure of direction, Cartier was even
more uncertain as to the dangers he faced. This was a
completely foreign region to him. To add to his doubt, he
began to recall vague tales and legends among the People.
There were, it was whispered, tribes to the south who ate
other people. It had seemed unimportant at the time, and
he had dismissed the subject as unlikely to be of concern
to him, beyond morbid curiosity.

Now, in the dark of night, he often wondered. He
wished he had more specifically determined *where* these

southern tribes of cannibals might be. If, indeed, there was any truth at all in the story.

More and more uneasy, he began to travel largely at night, sleeping through the day, and setting his direction by the stars. Once he saw that the trail he followed was becoming plainer and more traveled. He assumed that a settlement of some sort must be ahead, so he left the trail.

That night, from the top of the ridge, he watched the fires of a village, and successfully skirted around it. He did not know whether there was danger or not, but preferred not to find out in an unpleasant way.

When he finally did encounter someone, the circumstances were so bizarre that he could not have foreseen it. He had noticed, just a time or two, the hoofprints of an unshod horse in the soft portions of the trail. The country was hilly, but he could see that a horse might be of use here. The trail was open enough, and the areas of grassland more frequent. He began to look forward to the far horizons of the prairie, and to wonder how he might acquire a horse.

Shadows were lengthening, and he had just awakened preparing to begin his nightly trek. He was thinking about the possibility of a horse, when he heard an inquiring nicker. He jumped to the concealment of bushes along the trail, and waited. For a moment there was no sound. Then he heard the muffled clip-clop of a slowly moving horse approaching. He fitted an arrow to the bowstring.

Only one animal, from the sound, wandering at random. The hoofbeats stopped, and the animal was near enough that Cartier could hear the crisp sounds as it cropped grass along the trail. Still, caution was in order. Carefully, he peered through the bushes.

The horse was a well-built bay, saddled with a flat rawhide pad, and trailing the reins of a "war bridle," a thong knotted around the lower jaw. There was no evidence of a rider. Cartier watched from concealment. This could be a trap of some sort.

But no, the animal showed evidence of a heavy, lathering sweat. It had been running hard, but the sweat was now drying. There must have been an accident of some sort, or perhaps a fight. Maybe just a runaway.

He moved slowly from cover and spoke softly to the horse. It snorted with suspicion, but looked at him calmly with large, intelligent eyes. Moving slowly, he approached the animal, talking and crooning to it. Sing to it, Looks Far always advised.

The horse seemed to relax now, and Cartier cautiously picked up a dangling rein. The animal tensed with fear. It trembled and rolled white-rimmed eyes at him, but gradually quieted.

He examined the horse carefully. There seemed to be no injuries, only the drying lather of a hard run. Other than that, it was just what it had seemed. A young mare, perhaps three or four summers, recovering slowly from an extreme exertion.

Cartier stripped the saddle pad from the mare's back, and began to rub her down with handfuls of grass. He knew that to neglect this might stiffen overworked muscles, perhaps even do permanent harm.

As he worked, he pondered the situation. Here was the horse he badly needed, but he did not know what lay ahead. He had no desire to blunder into the night without further information. It was plain that the mare had been running from trouble of some sort. That trouble might be a threat to Cartier or might not, but there was no way of knowing. He dared not risk it. Still, there was no major advantage in staying where he was.

He finally decided on a compromise. Later, there would be a moon, a few days past full. He would wait the hour or two and let the mare rest and graze beside the trail. Then he would proceed cautiously, leading the mare rather than riding. When they came to a desirable place for a halt, he could stop until daylight, and then proceed.

Yes, that would be a good plan. He led the mare to grassy strip beside the trail, and squatted beside a tree to wait. He listened to the night sounds, and wondered a what might lie ahead on the trail.

To have run so hard, so frantically, the bay mare mus have been panicked somehow. It seemed unlikely that fight would produce such a reaction. Most horses woul not behave in that manner. Also, there was no indication of ceremonial paint. The horse had not been painted fo battle.

So, if a conflict was involved, it had been an accidenta meeting. Or, perhaps, merely an accident, injuring th rider. But why would that panic the horse, and send i running mindlessly away from the scene?

He arrived at another dead end. There was simply nothing he could think of that would produce this reac tion, given the facts he already had. The hair on the back of his neck bristled a little in questioning doubt. There was something here that he did not recognize, something dark and foreboding. The possibility of something super natural, some dread thing out there in the night, made his skin crawl. He was glad for the company of the bay mare.

He realized that he was at a disadvantage, in strange country, with no knowledge of its medicine or its spirits He must be very cautious.

Cartier drew a deep breath. Here he was, he realized thinking like one of the People, rather than like a civi lized European with a certain amount of education.

Well, why not? This was their country, as France was his. Was it not possible that the spirits were differen here? Not better or worse, but different?

He was beginning to believe that to survive in this vas new continent, it was necessary to think like the People It would enable him to read the signs and act accordingly He glanced up at the Seven Hunters and waited fo moonrise.

20

» » »

It was a long time before the rising of the moon. Cartier realized he had miscalculated. It seemed only a short while ago that the moon was full. He could not remember exactly. But yes, as he counted on his fingers, he realized the truth. Moonrise was approximately an hour later each night, and it had been several nights since the full moon rose at sunset.

He was not entirely reacclimated to the ways of the People, he decided. He could not imagine Red Feather, his wife's father, fretting impatiently while he waited for the moon to rise.

Finally the orange crescent of the half-moon crept slowly above the horizon. Impatiently, Cartier took the rein and led the mare down the trail in the direction from which she had come. He regretted a trifle having lost half a night's travel, but this was better. Better than blundering ahead into the unknown. He did not mind traveling in the dark, but when there was known trouble somewhere ahead, it would be foolhardy to ignore it. Besides, if he managed this situation carefully, he would have acquired a horse.

Leading the animal was tedious, and several times he thought of riding. Each time he decided against it. There was too much hazard in the possibility of low-hanging limbs, especially in the event of a runaway. Something had badly frightened the mare before. For Cartier to be on her back if she panicked again could be extremely dangerous in the woods.

So, he progressed slowly and cautiously, while the moon slid higher and the night became brighter. Once he stopped and waited while a cloud obscured the moon's face entirely for a time. Then he moved on.

The mare was cooperative, leading well and happily grazing when he stopped to reconnoiter. Therefore, when she began to react strangely, he was almost caught unawares.

The sky was graying in the east behind him, the first dull promise of the false dawn, when it happened. The mare suddenly snorted in alarm and bolted to run. The rein burned through his fingers, the knot at the end barely enabling him to hold on. The animal was attempting to run back in the direction they had come. She dragged him a few steps before he managed to jerk the war bridle and regain control. He led her a few more paces, talking quietly, and then paused.

The mare stood still, trembling as she tried to peer back at the area that seemed to generate her fear. Cartier petted and quieted the animal, talked and crooned, but the fear would not depart. He led down the back trail, pausing frequently until the mare seemed confident and calm. He found a quiet clearing and tied her securely. Then, in the growing light, he fitted an arrow to his bowstring and made his way back along the trail.

Cold chills crept up the back of his neck and made the hair stand. There was no way of knowing what he might be coming to. Something terrifying to a horse, at any rate. Something which had lost her rider and caused the mare to run blindly in a panic. He would have preferred to avoid this unknown danger, but saw no way. There appeared to be no trail but this that led in his direction.

The country was too rough to risk travel without some indication of a trail.

He moved slowly, the path winding through the trees. He kept his gaze roving from right to left as he moved, taking in the entire forest ahead, with an occasional glance backward. He saw nothing unusual.

This was not particularly reassuring. It made it seem likely that something supernatural was involved. He had heard that horses and dogs see and hear things that humans cannot. His palms were moist as he nervously shifted his hands on the bow.

He stopped, returned the arrow to its quiver, and slung the bow on his back. Then he took the ax from his waist to carry in his right hand. There was no special reason. It just seemed that he should have one hand free. He moved on along the trail.

It widened ahead, and there appeared to be a spring where travelers stopped for water. He saw nothing unusual, so he moved forward and stooped to drink. He sipped from a cupped hand, still warily looking around.

As he bent for more water, his eye fell on something that made him forget all about drinking. His hand reached for the ax, as he looked around the clearing. Those who had used the spring through the years had deepened and improved it by the addition of rocks around it. This ring of stone formed a pool for drinking.

On one of the stones, however, was a blotch of dried blood, spilling across the top surface and down one side. Cartier moved forward. He was no tracker, but he had been considered an apt pupil by the warriors of the People. Perhaps he could unravel the mystery.

Was this human blood? He searched the stone carefully. Yes, there, on the sharp corner, a couple of long, straight black hairs, glued down by the clotted blood. Human, beyond a doubt.

This, then, had probably been the rider of the runaway horse. If he had struck his head on this stone, he must have fallen from the horse, or been struck down. The blow on the head could have killed him, or not.

Once again, what could have terrified the horse and caused it to run? Puzzled, he began to search for more sign. There were several different moccasin tracks around the spring, mostly days old. Of the newer prints, he wondered which might have been made by the bay's rider. If, indeed, he had even dismounted before catastrophe struck. And what catastrophe?

Then he saw it. The print was in a muddy spot, half hidden by ferns and nearly against the rocky hillside where the spring emerged. A footprint like that of a flat-footed human, but with great claws on the toes. Bear!

He had seen horses go into complete panic at the mere scent of bear. That must be the answer here. The rider had approached the spring, and the horse had shied in terror at a chance meeting with a bear. Her rider had fallen and struck his head, while the mare bolted in panic.

But what then? Where was the body of the rider? Could the bear have dragged it away? He thought that over for a little while. If it had been the real-bear with silver-tipped fur, who walks erect like a man, it was possible. Maybe even likely. But this track was that of the black bear, smaller and less likely to drag away a carcass the size of a man.

No, the rider must have recovered consciousness, at least enough to drag himself away. The size of the puddle of dried blood indicated that he had lain there for some time. Possibly someone had come to help him.

Well, the mystery seemed solved. He stood, somewhat relieved, and hurried back to where he had left the mare. He untied the animal and led her back toward the trail. Now that he understood her problem, he could handle the situation. A firm hand and reassurance would carry the mare past the spot of her terrifying confrontation with the bear.

He tossed the rein over her neck and was reaching for his pack, when she gave a sudden snort of surprise. He followed the direction of her gaze.

A few steps away, completely blocking the trail, stood three well-armed warriors.

21

Cartier thought rapidly. He must not appear alarmed. He turned and made the hand sign for greeting, showing the unarmed right hand.

"Greetings, my brothers!" he began.

The others did not move, except that one nervously fingered the arrow already fitted to his bowstring.

"I am called Woodchuck, of the Elk-dog People," he offered. "How are you called?"

"You are called dead," signed one, with a sneer.

"Is this a way to greet a traveler?" Cartier signed in mock amazement.

He wondered if he could reach his ax before the first arrow struck.

"Such a traveler as you," sneered the other man. "You are a murderer."

"It is not true. I have killed no one."

Quickly, he evaluated the three. The one who was doing the sign talk, angry and vindictive, was not thinking clearly. He would have to calm down considerably to be effective. The man on his left appeared strong as an ox, but a trifle slow-witted.

The dangerous one was the third man, who kept nervously playing with the arrow. His narrow eyes glittered with unmistakable cruelty. If there is a chance at all, Cartier told himself, I must put him down.

"You are the killer of my brother," the man was signing again. "We found him yesterday. We were seeking his horse, but find his killer instead."

Now Cartier understood.

"No," he protested. "I have not seen your brother. I saw the place where he fell, at the spring. A bear frightened his horse, and I caught it on the trail."

"We saw no bear. You killed him and stole the horse."

"No. I will show you the bear's track."

He was stalling while he evaluated his chances, which seemed pretty slim. There was little chance he could convince them.

"We will kill you, then look for the bear," the man signed.

The other two laughed and nodded.

Cartier wondered if the bay mare was trained as the horses of the People. They mounted from the right side, while Europeans mounted from the left. If he could swing up, rush at the three men, and perhaps strike the dangerous one as he passed, there was a chance. Then he would have to worry about pursuit. He wondered whether these warriors had horses somewhere, or if they were on foot.

"Very well, we fight."

He placed his hand on his ax, very slowly.

"Which of you is first to die?"

There was laughter, but the attention of all three was riveted on Cartier.

Then he saw the slight hint of sinuous motion in the dust of the trail.

"My brothers," he signed very deliberately, "in the trail behind you is a real-snake."

"You lie. There is no snake. It is a trick."

"No. Look."

"And you attack when we turn."

91

The suspense was too much for the slow-witted one. He turned his head for a quick glance.

"*Aiee!*" he almost screamed.

It was the first word that had been voiced. The next sound was the warning buzz of the rattles. That was only brief, as the huge snake launched itself. Not at the man who had shouted, but at the one Cartier had marked as the dangerous one.

He tried to jump clear, but the fangs hooked into the muscle of his calf. The man screamed in pain, as the weight of the creature dragged from his injured leg. Frantically, he reached down to grasp the wriggling snake and throw it from him. It landed on a bush and slid quickly out of sight, down among the foliage.

Cartier had not been idle. He swung quickly to the mare's back and kicked her forward. Past the startled warriors, knocking them aside, while their companion writhed on the ground in agony.

"Thank you, Little Brother," he murmured in the direction where the snake had landed.

About a bow-shot down the trail, he was startled to see three horses tied. He paused, long enough to cut them loose, glancing backward for possible pursuit. He yelled at the animals and drove them ahead of him at a gallop.

As he had hoped, they thundered past the spring without pause. The bay mare, intent on following the others, shied only a moment as they passed.

He let her run for a while, then pulled her in, slowing first to a canter and then a trot to cool her down. He was pleased with the mare, her gaits all he could have hoped. Finally, they walked, and the mare's breathing steadied to normal.

They passed the loose horses, now grazing slowly along the trail. Cartier looked them over with a critical eye. There was a stocky roan that caught his fancy, but no. It was better to stick with a known quantity. He patted the bay on the neck and moved on.

He felt good about the encounter. He had his weapons,

nd had not even used them. It had been necessary to
bandon his pack, but it seemed a small loss. There was
othing that could not be replaced. His blanket was
olled and tied to the saddle pad.

And now, he had a horse. Only now, he realized how
much he had missed the exuberance that came with trav-
ling cross-country with a good horse between his knees.

Now, if he could only avoid further contact with the
ribe of the unfortunate rider who no longer needed his
ay mare.

How odd, he mused, that the medicine of the real-
nake whose life he had spared had now saved his own.
Ie nudged the horse ahead, still alert for trouble.

22

>> >> >>

There was a little trouble skirting around the village. The country was so rough and tree-covered that whenever he left the trail he became completely confused as to direction.

He had not realized that his year in open prairie had affected him so. He had always delighted in the shade of the ancient oaks in his homeland. Now he found the forest a hindrance to him. Periodically, he had to fight off the feeling of being trapped and enclosed by the surrounding foliage.

The first day he traveled very cautiously. If he could locate the village from which the three warriors had come, he could take better measures to avoid it. So far, he had not the faintest idea in which direction it lay. Except, of course, he knew it was not behind him. This thought stimulated another. The other side of the coin was, it must be ahead. If there was only this one trail on which he traveled, and the village was on a trail, it must be ahead.

But how far? The men he had encountered might be within half a day of home. They might just as easily be on a journey, several sleeps from their village. No, that was not likely. He had seen no packs, and their horses

94

had carried no supplies. At most, then, they were within a day of home.

At the thought, he stopped short. This was too dangerous. He might blunder into a hunter or some lovers out for a walk, before he realized that he was nearing the village. Somehow, he must get his bearings, and learn where the danger lay.

He dismounted, taking the rein to lead the mare off the trail. If he could reach higher ground, perhaps he could orient himself. The timber seemed not quite so dense to his left, and the gentle rise of the slope promised some sort of hill or ridge.

Cartier paused and studied the surrounding terrain, while the mare made use of the opportunity to graze. The morning was quiet. A couple of squirrels chased each other up and down the bole of an ancient oak tree.

At a little greater distance, he heard the alarm call of a pair of crows, which could be of some concern. Carefully, he moved in that direction. What had disturbed them? The timber thinned as he approached the summit of the hill. It was rounded and bald-topped, like a great grassy dome.

Cartier paused, still in the shelter of the oaks, and glanced back at the peacefully grazing horse. A flash of motion ahead caught his eye. Several crows came swooping over the knob, screaming accusingly. The object of their alarm was a sleepy-looking owl, pursued and harried by his traditional enemies. The crows were being joined by more, the screams of alarm growing with the pursuit.

Cartier smiled.

"*Kookooskoos*, you hunted too long this morning," he murmured.

The beleaguered owl was striving his utmost to reach the timber. Somewhere would be his lodge in a hollow tree, and safety from his tormentors. Cartier could sympathize. He felt pursued himself at the moment. The fortunate thing about this scene, however, was that it gave Cartier information. This normal activity, the crows' ha-

rassment of the great owl, indicated that there was no
human presence on the hilltop. Cartier moved ahead.

The view from the knob was magnificent, but he noted
that only in passing. There were more important, life-
and-death things to observe this morning. Quickly, he
swept the surrounding country.

There, some distance to the north, a gray smudge hung
over the trees. That would be from the cooking fires of
the village. It was well that he had left the trail.

To the west, the direction in which he hoped to travel,
the view was encouraging. He could see that the rough
terrain was beginning to flatten somewhat. The small,
conical hills which seemed almost random in their place-
ment gave way to low ridges. Areas of flatland could be
seen, some of them grassy meadows.

Cartier returned to the mare, swung up, and turned her
head to the west. Through that day, he moved cautiously, pausing at frequent intervals to reconnoiter the
country ahead.

His camp that night was a cheerless one, since he felt
uneasy about lighting a fire. His stomach told him that
he had not eaten since the previous evening, but there
was little he could do. His meager supply of dried meat
had been in the pack he had been forced to abandon.

At daylight, he woke and was preparing to start on,
when he saw a couple of fat cottontail rabbits playing
across the clearing. Carefully, he fitted an arrow, and
quickly dispatched one of the animals. The other scam-
pered to safety.

Now he was faced with a dilemma. He felt the urgency
to move on, but hunger gnawed at him. Besides, he must
do something with the meat immediately to prevent
spoilage. The day promised to be a warm one.

Even as he thought, he was kindling a small fire, choos-
ing only the driest of fuel to avoid smoke. He struck it
alive with flint and steel. He had never quite mastered
the technique of fire from the rubbing-sticks, which the
People used. Fortunately, his own fire-making equipment

had been in the pouch at his waist when he abandoned his pack.

While the fire gained strength, he skinned and gutted the rabbit, saving the skin. It was not of much use, but would do to wrap the cooked meat.

The rabbit was poorly cooked, in his haste to depart, but it was certainly better than the growling of an empty gut as he traveled. He wolfed down half the meat and wrapped the remainder in the skin, tucking it in his pouch. Then he scattered his fire and departed.

It was late that day that he encountered the hunters. He had stopped on a hilltop to scan the country ahead, and had seen nothing. He returned to his horse, mounted, and approached the hill again.

To his astonishment, he nearly collided with four riders approaching from the other side. They seemed as surprised as he, and all reined in nervously. There was no opportunity to run. He must bluff it out.

Quickly, he evaluated the situation. The men were well-armed, but wore no paint. That meant they were hunting or traveling, not ready for fighting. He knew they would be evaluating him, too. He raised his right hand in salute and began to sign.

"Greetings, my brothers! How is the hunting?"

His question was unanswered.

"Who are you? What is your tribe?"

"I am Woodchuck, of the Elk-dog People."

He pointed west.

"How are you here?"

"I have been far to the north, a place called Mishighan, and I am going home."

"Where is your pack?"

Careful, now, he thought. This must look real. He relaxed and chuckled.

"*Aiee*, that was a close escape! A bear frightened my horse, and scattered my supplies. I was fortunate to save my blanket. It was tied to the horse."

There was a sympathetic chuckle. These men could relate to this sort of problem. He took it a step further.

"I lost my food. I have had nothing to eat for two suns except half of this rabbit!"

He drew out the fur-wrapped bundle. The men were laughing now. It was going well, Cartier thought. Then one of the hunters gave a sudden exclamation and pointed to the horse. A heated discussion followed for a moment. Then the man who appeared to be the leader began to sign again.

"Where did you get this horse?"

Sweat began to dampen his palms. He must appear perfectly calm. He leaned forward and patted the bay on the neck.

"I traded my canoe for her when I left the Big River. Is it not a good one?"

He sat back, still smiling.

"It looks like the horse of my cousin, White Wolf," signed one of the other men.

"No, my friend. This is the horse of Woodchuck."

He continued to smile, but kept a hand ready to reach for the ax.

"It looks like Wolf's," insisted the other man.

Cartier leaned back as if to examine the animal more closely.

"I do not know White Wolf. He must have a good horse, too. But one bay looks much like another. I like a spotted horse, myself."

There were nods of agreement, so he continued.

"I once had a gray that was a good buffalo hunter. It was much like yours."

He pointed to the rangy gray gelding which the leader rode. In a few moments the entire group was relaxed again, talking horses. Then the leader turned to Cartier again.

"It grows late," he signed. "Will you camp with us tonight? We have meat."

23

» » »

Cartier had not hoped for anything like this much success in his conversation. From the point of suspicion, now these men were willing to visit, exchange opinions about horses, and generally welcome him to their campfire and their food. Even the one who had thought he recognized his cousin's horse soon dropped all hint of suspicion.

Actually, it became a rather enjoyable evening. Cartier made a big event of offering to share his half-eaten rabbit with the others. It was passed around the circle, with a couple of the men jokingly taking bites to assure the visitor of their appreciation.

One complained, in mock disappointment, that it was not well cooked. Cartier admitted his shortcomings.

"*Aiee*, I have never been able to cook well," he muttered sadly.

There was laughter.

"You need a woman," one man advised.

Cartier's depression returned.

"I had a wife," he said simply. "She was killed, five summers past."

The man next to him laid a sympathetic hand on Cartier's shoulder.

"My heart is heavy for you, my brother. But it is not good for a man to live alone. Another wife brings honor to the memory of your loss."

Soon the mood was lively again, as the broiling meat sizzled and began to appear nearly done. Cartier's belly growled in anticipation.

"Buffalo?" he asked.

"Yes. We killed a fat cow yesterday."

"Where is your home?" asked Cartier, still somewhat unsure about these companions.

"That way," one signed, pointing northwest. "Three sleeps."

Cartier relaxed somewhat. The party had been traveling east, or southeast. That meant they were coming from their own village, three days journey away. They had not yet come to the area where he had acquired the mare.

"You are far from home," he signed casually. "You are hunting?"

"Yes," one man shrugged. "We will also visit another village of our tribe. Slim Otter wishes it."

One of the other young men was staring self-consciously at the fire, but smiling to himself.

"Otter has a woman he wishes to visit," contributed another man.

"It is good," signed Cartier.

"Come with us. Maybe we find a woman for you, too, Woodchuck."

There was general laughter.

"No, no," Cartier signed with a smile. "I am traveling the other way. I wish to see my son."

There were nods of agreement.

He was thinking rapidly. There was every possibility that the village they would visit was that of the unfortunate previous owner of the mare. If the horse had actually been that of the cousin, White Wolf, Cartier must strive to be far away before they discovered it.

There was a moment when his basic honesty surfaced. If he told them the story, the true facts about the horse, the unfortunate rider, the bear, and the real-snake, surely these friendly men would believe him and understand. But no, they would insist that he accompany them, to verify the facts. That would lose him much time, and be dangerous besides. The men he had encountered before, friends and relatives of the dead man, would never understand.

Best that he say nothing, he decided. It bothered him a little that these men who had befriended him and shared their food would later believe him to be a liar, a horse thief, and a murderer, but it could not be helped.

The pace at which the broiled hump ribs were devoured was slowing now. The men sat belching comfortably.

"Tell us, Woodchuck, where did your people come from?" one signed.

It was the time for telling of stories, exchange of legends and myths of each so that the others might enjoy.

"We are people of the wide skies," Cartier signed formally. "Skin lodges, moving from place to place."

The others nodded.

He tried to recall how the creation story of the People was told. There was a joke on the listeners, if he could remember how to tell it properly.

"The People came from the center of the earth. The Old Man of the Shadows sat astride a hollow cottonwood log, and tapped on it with a drum stick."

He paused to pantomime the slow cadence of the tapping stick.

"Each time he tapped, another person crawled through into this world."

He paused. This was the place to pause and wait for the joke. He had seen Pale Star do it many times. The four listeners waited, the silence growing heavier.

"Well," one man finally signed. "Are they still coming through?"

"No," Cartier answered sadly. "It is unfortunate. A fat

101

woman got stuck in the log, and no more have come through since. That is why the tribe is small."

There was general laughter, directed at the one who had asked the question. Now it would be polite to ask the story of the others. The sharing of creation stories was a favorite topic for the story fires.

"What is your story?"

The men looked at each other, and pointed to the one who appeared to serve as the group's leader. He began to sign.

"In the long-ago times, our people were far to the north. The First Ones, brothers, three of them, came up out of a big lake. They found wives, and were the fathers of the three clans of our tribe. There have been other splits since."

Obviously, this was not the best storyteller in the tribe. But then, Cartier recalled, neither was he the best storyteller of the People. However, he had watched and listened to Pale Star, one of the best. He had seen her use several languages, including French and the tongue of the People. She had also used sign talk. On their journey five summers ago, they had encountered several tribes whose languages she did not know. Her stories had still entranced her audience. Lieutenant Du Pres also had become adept at storytelling under her urging.

He, Woodchuck, had always felt reluctant to participate. He had felt shy about being the center of attention. Now, somehow, he was enjoying this story fire. He was pleased to be able to tell the stories of the People.

Cartier stopped short, startled at himself. Without realizing it, he had thrown himself into the story exchange wholeheartedly. But the stories he was telling were not those of his own French background. They were those of his wife's tribe. He had considered himself so much a part of the People that he had not even noticed. His own culture had been forgotten as he told of his adopted tribe.

Ah well, it was no matter.

"How does your tribe say the spotted cat lost his tail?" one of the others signed.

"It was like this," Cartier began. "In the long-ago times, spotted cat had a long tail, like the real-cat. Then one day, a hunter was passing by, so spotted cat hid in a hollow tree. Except, it was not an ordinary tree, but The Old Man in disguise. He could become a tree, or a rock—"

Overhead, the Seven Hunters wheeled slowly around the Real-star, and the men around the fire fixed their attention on every motion of the storyteller.

24

» » »

In the ensuing days, Cartier thought much about the men whose campfire he had shared. Their fellowship had been a warm, pleasant interlude. They were men who understood his problems, and shared his frustrations.

He felt the pangs of guilt again that he had been forced to deceive them. Yet, if he had not, he might be lying dead somewhere at this moment. Instead he was traveling well on a good horse, with a small pack of buffalo meat tied behind him. His erstwhile companions had insisted on sharing their food with him.

He hoped that when the story of the death of White Wolf came to the ears of these men, their minds would remain open, and their hearts good toward him. He no longer had any doubt at all that White Wolf had been the owner of the bay mare.

There was the possibility, of course, that relatives of the dead man would come seeking vengeance. Perhaps he should have given the hunters misleading information as to who he was, and of what tribe. No, he could not have done it. His story had been as near the truth as he could manage under the circumstances. He could not have done otherwise. It was not in his friendly, easygoing nature.

It had been difficult to deceive them at all. It is hard to lie to someone with whom you have shared food and the warmth of a campfire.

He rode on, trying to put distance between them. There would be less reason for concern with each day of travel.

Cartier skirted around the village. The men he had camped with had urged him to stop there for supplies, but he did not feel right about it. That would be carrying his deceit a step further, and it already lay heavy on his conscience. Some men could cheerfully have carried it off, he knew. Perhaps some would even revel in the chicanery of it all, but it was not in his makeup.

Carefully, he avoided all contact, making a cold camp one night. He even went hungry for a day, rather than stop to hunt. Then, satisfied that he was past all but a chance encounter, he moved on westward with more confidence.

The country still appeared completely unfamiliar. He had never been this far south before. He wondered if his direction was correct. Should he bear farther north as he traveled?

It was no matter, he finally decided. He would come to the open prairie eventually, and find someone to inform him of the People's whereabouts. He traveled on, heading just a bit north of due west.

There was much time to think. He pondered at great length about the curious event where he had been saved by the real-snake. *Mon dieu*, what did it mean? There had been a moment, there, when he had felt confidence in his communication with the creature. He seemed to have complete knowledge of what was about to happen, even *when* the snake would strike. It seemed to imply the repayment of a debt, when he had spared the life of the other snake. Or, was that the same snake? No, of course not. That was many days' journey away.

Then why did he feel the feeling so strongly? He longed to reach the People, to ask Looks Far about the meaning of this experience. There *was* meaning, somehow. Of that, he was certain.

It was many days yet before he reached the village of the Growers, where he finally asked directions. He was concerned that when he did contact them, he would have nothing to trade for supplies. The main exchange by the People consisted of meat and robes for the Growers' corn, beans, and dried pumpkin.

Perhaps he could manage to make a kill and carry meat to a village. Still, he had no way to transport meat for much distance. A deer might be loaded on the horse while Cartier walked, but that did not seem a desirable turn of events. What he really craved was the tender hump ribs of buffalo, anyway.

He killed enough for his own needs as he traveled, mostly small game, once a deer. He camped for three days, attempting to dry part of the meat, but the weather would not cooperate. The climate seemed damp and muggy compared to the open skies of the prairie. He wondered how the tribes who lived in the area preserved their food. Smoke, perhaps, as some of the river tribes did with the fish that formed a staple of their diet. He experimented with that theory, but was reluctant to build a smoky fire. Slow drying over a fire of dry wood seemed the likeliest method.

Even that experiment ended when a summer storm swept across the hills and all but quenched his cooking fire. Irritated, he ate all he could hold, rolled some of the partly cooked venison and a supply of fresh meat in the skin, and traveled on.

He was a bit ashamed, then amused at himself for his impatience. Why should it matter? He had rested, eaten, he had food, and he was traveling again. He chuckled and touched a heel to the flank of the bay mare.

The country was opening up now, and the areas of grassland were larger and more frequent. He saw the village from a great distance. The cultivated plots of corn and beans made splotches of different shades of green.

Yes, here he could stop for information. More importantly, as he looked to the west, he could see buffalo. A scattered herd, grazing quietly across the green of an expanse of grassland. At this distance, their color was blurred. The slowly moving specks were not distinguishable as animals of any particular color. They were merely contrasting spots of some nondescript dark shade, brown, black, or gray against the smooth green.

Cartier studied the situation. Yes, it might work. It would take half the day to maneuver around a portion of the herd, but the day was young. If the buffalo could only be made to move in the direction he wished, it could be done.

He considered going first to the village to try to enlist help, but abandoned the thought immediately. His scheme might not work, and to attempt to organize a hunt would take time. No, he would try it alone. If the buffalo moved sufficiently well, and came close to the village, their hunters should be alert enough to take advantage of the situation.

If not—well, he could make a kill or two, then go and invite them to come and share his meat. It should occur close enough to the village for that.

He lifted the reins and clucked to the bay mare as he turned her head to the west.

25

Sometimes, for reasons beyond the understanding of mere mortals, things go well. There were any number of reasons why Cartier's plan might have failed. A chance shift of the breeze, an unexpected noise, the flutter of a bird, might have set the buffalo in motion. Motion was all to the good if it took place in the right direction. It would be equally bad, he realized, if the animals ran in panic away from the village.

Carefully he skirted the herd, taking care that the wind direction was correct. It was a slow maneuver, and he wished profoundly to be on with it. But, he realized, he *must* be patient. The entire success of the scheme revolved around his patience for the next little while.

A wary old cow lifted her head to stare at him, nervously twitching her tail. Cartier pulled the bay mare to a stop and waited. He knew that the cow would be testing the air for scent of the newcomer. Her vision was far less acute than her smell. The heartbeats ticked past, and the cow remained still, so Cartier continued to do likewise. A grasshopper with orange wings clattered past and landed near a clump of sumac. The buffalo appeared to interpret this sound as evidence of normality, and resumed grazing.

Gently, Cartier nudged the mare forward, approaching a yearling bull. The youngster moved aside and drifted away, only mildly annoyed. He repeated the process on another animal, then another. Soon a dozen or more animals were moving in the desired direction, pausing to graze, taking a few steps, pausing again.

This would be the tricky part. If one of the buffalo became suspicious or turned the wrong way— No, he must avoid such thoughts. The creatures *would* move in the desired direction, he insisted to himself, throttling his doubts while they were yet unborn.

Very gradually, he worked his little herd away from the others. Now, without distraction, he pushed a little faster. It would be important now, to choose the right moment. He must initiate a charge unexpectedly, causing the animals to bolt as a group away from him. Hopefully, toward the village.

He also hoped that someone in the village was alert and watching the buffalo approach. He could see evidences in the distance of the cultivated crops, showing their various shades of green. There was another thing to provide risk to him, he thought. The Growers might be quite irritable if he drove buffalo through their corn field.

Yes, it would be better to make his move now. He kicked the bay. The startled horse leaped forward and the buffalo began to run. Cartier fitted an arrow and let it fly into a soft flank just behind the rib cage. The bull faltered and dropped behind. Cartier chose another animal and the mare flattened her ears and drove forward in pursuit. He let fly and missed.

They were now approaching a fringe of trees which grew along a tiny stream. The uneven terrain would slow the buffalo, but could make footing treacherous. He could loose one more shot before they reached the creek. He fitted the arrow, drew it to its head, and this time he did not miss.

The air was heavy with the dust of running buffalo, obscuring the leaders ahead. For this reason, he nearly failed to see the herd start to turn. Then he heard yells and saw the sweep to the left. People in the trees and along the creek bed were shooting as the animals veered away.

Cartier pulled his horse to the left, following the swing of the herd, and drove another arrow to its mark. He saw another animal go down, felled by a bowman in the creek.

He began to pull his mare to a slower canter, circling back away from the remnants of the herd. There were enough buffalo down. The bay was still excited, dancing and sidestepping.

"Ah, ma'm'selle, you have hunted buffalo before!" Cartier murmured, patting the sweaty neck. The horse had done well.

She was still blowing hard, nostrils flaring with exertion and excitement. He drew her in, still circling, until at length she consented to a fast walk. They approached several men who were emerging from concealment along the stream, laughing and talking excitedly. One waved to the newcomer.

Cartier rode up to the cluster of bowmen, who seemed curious, although unconcerned.

"Greetings, my brothers," he signed. "I have brought meat."

There was general laughter.

"How are you called?" one asked.

"Woodchuck, of the Elk-dog People," he responded. "I am going home."

There were nods, and a short discussion.

"Your people are farther west," one of the men observed.

"Yes, I know. But I have never been this way before. Where is the River of Swans?"

Again, brief discussion.

"Northwest, maybe. We can talk later."

People from the village were straggling out to begin the butchering.

"I have three kills out there," Cartier signed. "They are yours. I only wish a little food for traveling."

The men nodded, and one called to two women who were passing. He apparently explained the situation, and pointed to the remaining arrows in Cartier's quiver. One of the women stepped over, glanced at the arrows, and nodded in understanding as she moved away.

Cartier knew that she would identify his kills by the painted markings, and would also return his arrows. He regretted the loss of the one arrow which had missed its mark. But such was the luck of the hunt.

Some time later, he sat on a robe by the fire and conversed with the chiefs of the village.

"We do not know your River of Swans," one was signing. "We might call it by another name as it flows through our country."

"But my tribe?"

"Oh yes. We know the Elk-dog People. A proud and mighty people."

There were nods of general agreement.

"Do you know where any of them are camped?"

"No, only that they are to the west and northwest. Your people seldom come this far to the east, except in seasons when there is little rain and poor hunting."

"Is it not time for their Great Council?" another man asked.

Cartier mentally counted the months. Yes, this was probably late in June, the Moon of Roses. Possibly even July, the Moon of Thunder. The People would have gathered at some favorite council spot for the Sun Dance and Big Council.

"Yes," Cartier agreed. "But I do not know. I have been gone for five seasons."

The others shook their heads in sympathy.

"Does anyone know where the Council is to be?" Cartier asked.

There were only blank looks. This village was a bit too far from the traditional territory of the People.

"It does not matter," he signed. "I will find them later."

"Yes," the chief agreed. "But now, the food is ready."

Women were bringing freshly cooked meat, with a mixture of stewed corn and beans. Cartier looked forward to the meal. It was several days since he had had any really good food, prepared with skill. As he freely admitted, his own cooking left much to be desired.

26
» » »

He spent several days with the Growers. During his year with the People, he had noted a general disregard for people who lived in permanent villages. There were slurring remarks about the smell of permanent dwellings, constructed partly in the ground. Also mentioned had been the idea that people who lived in such dwellings might have more lice and other parasites.

Therefore, it was gratifying to Cartier to find that these were friendly and hospitable people. He was not really deceived. He knew that a part of his welcome depended on the fact that he had assisted them in acquiring a great deal of meat, not to mention skins. His reception would have been considerably cooler, Cartier suspected, if he had arrived as a traveler with nothing, begging a handout.

But under the circumstances, he was welcomed royally. People could not show enough appreciation. Several of the women informed him the first evening that they would prepare and dry a portion of the meat for him to carry on his journey. Since that process would take a few days, he relaxed to wait. He would have preferred to be on the trail, but saw no way to accomplish it.

So he waited. It was not at all unpleasant to sit in the shade, smoke occasionally, and whittle. Once more his skill with the knife made him popular. He produced an assortment of small objects, from willow whistles for the children to fetishes and medicine-sticks for the more prestigious of his new acquaintances.

He slept outside, not entirely unmindful of the People's theory regarding lice among the Growers. The weather was pleasant anyway, and he was enjoying the taste of the beginning of open country.

Aside from his wish to be traveling, there was one nagging thought that kept occurring to him. What about the relatives of White Wolf, whose horse Cartier now rode? His conscience still bothered him a little over that entire event. In all fairness, though, how could he have handled it differently? He found himself hard to convince. In his mind, he relived the scene with the rattlesnake again and again. No, he could not have lingered. There would have been no convincing those warriors of his sincerity. The snake had saved him.

Additionally, while he waited, he wondered about the relatives of the dead White Wolf. The cousin, for instance, who had challenged Cartier's possession of the horse. Sometimes he wondered if even now, he might be followed by embittered relatives intent on vengeance.

He was glad when the day came to depart. As kind and generous as these Growers were, it was good to feel the horse under him. He took great lungfuls of the prairie air, and approached each hill in expectation of the far horizon beyond.

The country was more open with each day. Now great expanses of prairie became the dominant feature of the landscape. He altered his course slightly, moving more to the north. Without understanding why, he had a feeling that the River of Swans lay to the north.

A day after this change in direction, he began to experience a strange feeling that he was being watched. It was strong enough to make him stop and conceal the horse in a little gully. He spent some time on a hilltop, scanning the distant prairie in all directions. He saw nothing suspicious. A handful of buffalo grazed undisturbed, and a pair of buzzards soared high above, wheeling great circles on motionless wings. He watched the birds for a little while, but decided they were merely scouting for carrion, not watching anything in particular.

He was about to go on, when he caught sight of a dark speck on the distant prairie to the east. He studied it at length without coming to any conclusions. It could be a small tree or bush on the hillside. Distance would blur the green, making it indistinguishable. It might be a buffalo, or some other animal, or perhaps merely a rocky outcrop. Then too, it could be a horseman, or even a warrior on foot. There were moments when he would have sworn there were two objects that he watched.

If, thought Cartier, if I only had a spyglass. He stared until his vision blurred with the shimmering heat waves of distance, rubbed his eyes, and stared again. Then he remembered a hunt, long ago with the People. Someone, to see a long distance with clarity, had loosely closed a fist, and then peered through the tunnel made by the palm and fingers.

Cartier tried it, and was startled to see the increased clarity of distant objects. He placed the other hand also, and found that a longer tube was even better.

However, he could still not distinguish much that was of help to him. He could not even tell whether the speck was moving. What was it, the trick with two twigs that the People used?

Cartier reached for his knife and cut a sumac stem that was within easy reach, then cut it in two. One half he sharpened and thrust into the ground at arm's length in front of him. Lying on his belly, he sighted across the top of the stick at the distant speck. The other peg he pushed into the ground near his face, in exact line with the first. It took some careful adjustment to align the sticks precisely.

Finally, he was ready. He could look across the tops of the two twigs to see the speck in question, apparently sitting on the tips of his markers. Now, he could look again in a few moments and see if the pattern remained the same. If there had been any slightest bit of motion in the distant object, the sight pattern would no longer be aligned.

Cartier, pleased with himself, lay back to wait a little. While he waited, he peered again through his hands. Yes, now he was certain. There were two of the objects. Impatiently, he rolled to squint across the twigs.

The double speck was no longer aligned, but now appeared to the left of its original position. Cartier watched, fascinated. The course and motion, at a deliberate rate, suggested that the traveler had far to go. Probably not an animal, who would have paused to graze or look around. No, the speed of travel was highly suggestive of a man on foot. Or men, of course. If his impression of the double speck was correct, there were two of them, walking one behind the other.

Of one thing he was sure. He was being followed.

27

» » »

It took a little while for the importance of this development to come to full realization. Cartier watched the two with all the fascination of a bird stalked by a snake.

There was actually a sense of relief. He had worried and wondered about the possibility, and now it had become reality. The thought even crossed his mind that perhaps the marquis had sent someone after him as a deserter, to drag him back to justice. But no, he thought not. This would be White Wolf's family, bent on justice. He knew now the chilling fear that the aging buffalo bull feels when the wolves move in to follow his faltering trail.

He shook his head. No, he must not think such thoughts. Now that he was aware of his pursuers, he could defend himself. It was tempting to ride away. His horse would enable him to outdistance the pursuers on foot. But that would accomplish nothing. They had been relentless this far. No, it was time for the showdown.

Cartier glanced around the landscape. The warriors were following a wandering game trail, the one he himself had been traveling. They were undoubtedly tracking his horse's hoofprints and spoor. He might leave the trail for the tall grass, but the pursuers would then realize that they had been seen. If he could prevent their learning that one fact, he would have an advantage.

He slid backwards to conceal himself from view behind the ridge, and glanced around. It was plain that someone had rested here, from the matting of the grass. Very well, let that be plain. He removed the two pegs he had used for sighting and tossed them into a clump of dense brush. That would have been a sign too easy to interpret.

The fact that he had hidden the horse while he rested was too obvious to conceal. Well, so be it. If the warriors behind him wanted to take the time to unravel that fact, he could not prevent it.

He mounted the horse and boldly crossed the ridge, not even looking back. His skin crawled with the certain knowledge that there were eyes fixed on his back. It was necessary, however, to avoid the appearance that he now knew he was followed.

Once out of sight of those intent on vengeance, his demeanor changed. He began to search for a site for the ambush. Ahead of him, a low ridge presented a possibility. The trail led upward across a broken, rocky slope, crossing the ridge through a notch of saddle. That would be the spot. He could hide behind one of the rocks, and shoot as the warriors came up the trail.

He rode carefully, in a casual manner, so that his pursuers would see nothing amiss in his horse's trail. When he had crossed the ridge, he hurried to find a place of concealment for the horse. There was no ideal place, but he selected a fringe of trees along a stream, hobbled the mare, and left her to graze while he hurried back. He should still have time, he estimated.

There was still a wait after he had taken his position behind a well-situated rock. He was pleased with himself as he readied his weapons.

Strange, though, he thought as he waited. There were a few things he had not considered. Why, for instance, were the pursuers on foot, knowing that they followed a fugitive on horseback? In fact, *how* had they followed him this far, through many days of travel? He should have been putting more distance between them with each passing day. Instead, the warriors were here, now, hot on his trail. Even counting the days spent with the Growers, that should not be.

A chill of fear gripped him. There was something here that he did not understand. Was this some other enemy that now stalked him? Cartier glanced around nervously. He was not afraid of danger. He had faced that many times. This was different. He did not know the enemy, his purposes or what grudge he might carry. Fear of the unknown made his neck hairs stand and dampened his palms.

Perhaps he should postpone the confrontation until he knew more. Yes, that would be wise. He could quietly move back toward his horse before the warriors came in sight, and watch them for a day or two, if need be. They were taking a long time to cross the ridge.

He cast one last glance at the back trail before he made his move. A figure was just coming in sight. He waited a moment. There was still a good chance that he might slip away unseen. When the second warrior came in sight, he would move at a crouch until he crossed the ridge, then run.

The warrior plodded deliberately along the trail, apparently unconcerned. Cartier could tell little about him, except that he was slight of build. Probably a youth on his first war party. His teacher should advise him to be more alert.

A warning began to buzz, deep in Cartier's brain. Something was wrong. Two men would not comprise a war party. What, then, could be happening?

This doubt had scarcely risen before another fairly exploded in his consciousness. In his preoccupation with the young warrior, now halfway down the slope, he had forgotten the other man. That would be the one with experience, the leader and instructor. And that one had not yet crossed the ridge.

A moment of fright swept over him. He had, he thought, set a clever ambush for those who pursued him. Now, suddenly, he was the one in danger of being trapped. The young warrior across the valley was a decoy, to attract his attention. While he was thus occupied, the other man could have been . . .

In a sudden panic, Cartier jumped to his feet and sprinted over the ridge. It did not matter whether the young warrior saw him or not. He was well beyond the range of a bow-shot.

Then he slowed. He must be careful until he knew the whereabouts of the other man. Stepping quickly but cautiously, he circled toward the brushy draw where the horse was hobbled. He wasted a little time trying to stay in concealment, and finally came forth into the open.

Irritably, he noticed that the horse had wandered away from the spot where he had left her. He should have tied her by the war bridle, he accused himself, not the hobbles. But he had wanted to allow her to graze. The loosely applied front leg hobble would let the animal move a short distance, but not far, and only at a slow walk.

He turned upstream, and soon found that his way was blocked by a rocky slope with tangled brush. The mare would not graze in that direction.

Increasingly uneasy, he turned downstream. There was no sign of the bay mare. Could she have crossed the stream? He moved along the bank, looking for a spot where a hobbled animal might cross the streambed.

Yes, there, he thought. Just ahead was a place where a game trail, following the course of least resistance, led across a gravel bar and up the other bank. He hurried forward.

There were hoofprints in the damp soil, but another sign sent a wave of fear and then anger over him. A single moccasin print, possibly even placed there intentionally as an insult, told the story. He had been duped, completely and expertly. While the young warrior occupied his attention, the other man had circled and stolen the horse.

Now, Cartier felt, his troubles were just beginning. He was on foot, without supplies, which were still packed on the horse. Worse yet, his enemy was now mounted, and he still did not know who they were or why they followed him.

28

» » »

His thoughts were racing, wildly for a moment, and then settling to more useful directions. He must evaluate his predicament.

As far as he knew, there were only two of the enemy who pursued him. One was now mounted on the bay mare. The other would still be . . . That was it! If he could reach the man on foot, he could question him, hold him hostage, or kill him, even, to equalize the odds in this strange contest.

Before the thought was even finished, he was sprinting back up the slope to the ridge. He paused before he looked over, to ready himself for action.

About a bow-shot away, the young man sat on a boulder, waiting. Quickly, Cartier scanned the area. If his theory was correct, the other warrior would be returning at any moment.

The young warrior seemed to be watching to the north. A fold in the ridge gave a hint as to how the other man had circled unseen. He would be returning by the same path.

Even as Cartier watched, the bay came into view, loping easily with her rider urging her forward. He must reach the man on the rock first.

As he ran, he tried to evaluate the weapons of the more inexperienced warrior. There was no evidence of a bow, or an arrow quiver. The young man might have a spear or lance beside him on the ground, but Cartier saw none. The risk would be from an ax or club, possibly a knife. He raced forward, realizing that he would be there well before the horseman.

The rider yelled a warning, and the young warrior turned, appearing to see Cartier for the first time. Eyes wide with fright stared in terror at the approaching Cartier. To his amazement, he saw that this was no warrior at all, but a girl. She was hardly more than a child, though tall and gangly.

Now thoroughly confused, Cartier still realized the advantage that would result from her capture. The child darted away, and he dropped his bow to pursue her. Even then, the girl's quickness nearly caused him to lose her. He lunged in a flying leap and caught a slim ankle. The girl fell heavily, but before he could pinion the flying arms and legs, she twisted and struck out at him. From somewhere she had produced a flint knife, and Cartier felt the weapon slash across his thigh, slitting leggings, skin, and flesh. He caught a glimpse of blood welling up in the slash before they rolled in the struggle. He pinned the knife hand and jerked the weapon away from her, angry and hurting. Behind him, hoofbeats told of the approach of the warrior on the bay.

His best defense was possession of the girl. Twisting an arm behind her, he rolled to sit up with the hostage in front of him, the knife at her throat. He did not know if the bluff would work, but it was all he had.

The horse slid to a stop, and the rider glared in hatred. Cartier was once more astonished. This warrior was a woman, a young, very attractive woman.

"Do not kill her," the woman signed. "I will give you the horse."

With his free hand he pointed to a nearby bush, and made a tying motion. The woman swung down obediently and led the horse to the bush, where she tied the rein.

The situation could still be dangerous, Cartier realized. This woman was clever and bold. He was somewhat puzzled that he saw no weapons except a belt knife and the little knife that the girl had carried. What were a woman and child doing alone on the prairie. Or, were they alone? He risked a quick look around, but saw nothing.

He motioned the woman to move away from the horse, and she did so. He rose, still holding the girl.

"Let her go!" she signed.

He shook his head. He could not give up his advantage yet. His bow and arrows were lying in the grass behind him. He could not allow the woman to realize that possibility.

Carefully he began to back up the slope, followed by the woman.

"Stay back," he warned.

She continued to follow, but not so closely.

Cartier arrived at his weapon and stopped a moment to consider. If he released the girl, it was conceivable that the woman might try to take the child and make a run for the horse.

"That way," Cartier motioned.

He must maneuver this woman as best he could to avoid a dangerous situation. She moved in the indicated direction.

So far, none of the three had spoken a word. All communication had been in hand-sign talk. Cartier had had several surprises this day, but the biggest was yet to come. The woman spoke, a single phrase. It was one he had heard before. A vile, obscene expression of extreme insult. He could understand such feelings, under the circumstances. His astonishment was not at that, but that the obscenity was in the language of the People.

"You are of the People?" he blurted in amazement.

Now it was the young woman's turn to be astonished.

"You speak my tongue? Who are you?"

"I am Woodchuck, of the Southern band."

"*Aiee!*" The woman relaxed and laughed, a delightful rippling laugh. "I remember! The friend of Sky-Eyes."

"Yes," he agreed, releasing the girl. "And you?"

"Yellow Head."

Yes, a good name, he thought. This is a bright and handsome woman, like the bright blackbird with the yellow cape over its head and shoulders.

"How is it that you are here?" he asked. "Is this your daughter?"

"Yes. She is called Sunflower. We were captured by some of the Forest People, two summers ago. We have escaped. We go home."

"But you have no weapons."

Yellow Head looked at him a little indignantly.

"A woman of the People is not helpless."

He could agree to that. She had very nearly outwitted and outmaneuvered him. It was mostly luck that at this very moment he was not afoot and without supplies.

"Where do you go?" the woman asked.

"Back to the People. I left when my wife was killed."

"Yes, I remember. It was a sad time."

He felt the old pangs, but found himself better able to accept sympathy now.

"Which is your band?"

"We, too, are of the Southern band," Yellow Head answered.

"Good. We will travel together. Have you eaten today?"

"No."

"Let us camp. I have food."

They moved back over the ridge and into the level area along the creek. How fast things could change, Cartier reflected, as he opened his pack and Sunflower foraged for firewood along the brush on the slope.

29

» » »

Travel became more complicated with the woman and her daughter. There was only one horse, and three of them. Yellow Head had demonstrated her skill as a horse-woman in the bold scheme that had nearly left Cartier on foot. Now, however, she flatly refused to ride. It would seem inappropriate to her, he realized, to ride while he walked.

Cartier, in turn, did not feel comfortable about riding while the two women walked. The final outcome was that most of the time the girl, Sunflower, rode the horse while the two adults walked.

Sunflower was perhaps eleven or twelve summers, he estimated. She had not yet attained the bloom of sexual maturity, but had begun the sudden spurt of growth that lent stature to the women of the People. She was athletic, agile, and boyish in her movements. It was easy to see, as he watched the girl, how he could have mistaken her for a young warrior. His injured thigh reminded him as he walked that the impression was not completely inaccurate.

Once, in fact, on their first day of travel together, it was necessary to stop. The wound had opened and blood was trickling down his leg to puddle in his moccasin.

Yellow Head cut a strip from his blanket and bound the thigh tightly.

"I am sorry about the wound," she murmured self-consciously. "I will mend your legging when we stop to-night."

"It is nothing," he shrugged.

"But Sunflower might have killed you."

Cartier smiled.

"Yes, but she did not know. I might have killed either of you."

That evening by the fire she raised a question.

"Do you know where the Southern band is camped?"

"No. I do not know where any of them are. It is past the time for the Sun Dance, I think."

"Yes," she agreed. "How will you find them?"

"I will look for the Eastern band. They are usually near the River of Swans. I will ask the Growers."

"But you said you are of the Southern band."

"Yes, but my wife was of the Eastern band. We will stop with her parents."

"Ah yes, I remember now. Pale Star kept your son for a season. Then he went with Red Feather's lodge."

This was new information, received eagerly by Cartier. He had not known for certain where the boy was growing up.

"You have seen him? He is well?"

"No, no, Woodchuck. Remember, we have been away from the People for two seasons."

He was embarrassed to have forgotten such a thing, absorbed in his own problems.

"Tell me," he asked, hoping to make amends, "how were you captured?"

A look of sadness came over her face.

"We were camped farther east than usual. Game was scarce. Two men, my husband and another, made a buffalo kill some distance from camp. The two families were butchering out the meat when the war party came."

She paused and took a long breath.

"They killed everyone but Sunflower and me. Some wanted to kill us too, but their leader wanted me. I used that to bargain for Sunflower's life."

Cartier said nothing.

"I was a good wife," she continued, "and did all that they wished. I waited until the right time."

"And then?"

"I killed Black Bow, and hid his body. We helped search for him, and then ran away."

Her story was at an end. There was little that could be said in comment, though Cartier was certain she had left much untold.

"And you have traveled since?"

"Yes. We could take only a little food without suspicion, but we caught rabbits as we traveled."

Cartier knew that among the first lessons learned by a child of the People was the use of throwing sticks to hunt small game. Even so, to start such a journey, encumbered with a child, with a scant food supply and no weapons except knives took great courage. This was truly a remarkable woman.

"Tell me, what was your husband's name?"

"It is bad medicine to speak the name of the dead, Woodchuck."

"Of course. I am sorry."

"No, it is all right. I can use sign talk."

She made the signs for "yellow" and "horse."

"Ah yes. I knew him. We hunted together."

He wondered how he had failed to be aware of the pretty wife of Yellow Horse. But, he recalled, he had been newly married to Pink Cloud, and had thought of little else during that entire year.

"Yes," she said simply.

"Your husband was a good man."

"Yes."

"Yellow Head, let us talk of other things. What of Sky-Eyes and Pale Star?"

She brightened.

"Of course. You have not seen them since you left. Did you know they have a daughter? Now, also a son."

She counted on her fingers.

"*Aiee*," she said, almost to herself. "Three summers, now."

"They have only the two?"

"Yes, unless, of course, since I have been gone. No, I think not."

Sunflower returned with an armful of sticks and dumped them to the ground.

"You have only Sunflower?" Cartier asked.

"Yes," she replied, a little sadly. "Another child, a boy, died when he was small."

Cartier, kind and sympathetic by nature, was deeply touched by the woman's story. What a tragic, frustrated life! Knowing how deeply his own bereavement had affected him, he had the greatest of admiration for Yellow Head's invincible spirit. He had not handled his own grief nearly so well.

"My heart is heavy for you," he mumbled self-consciously.

She smiled.

"That was long ago, Woodchuck. I have tasted the ashes and have mourned. Now, I go on."

Sunflower now sat by the fire, chewing a strip of dried meat.

"Will we see anyone tomorrow, Woodchuck?"

"I do not know, little one. We will see."

The innocent question stirred his thoughts profoundly. They were nearing the country of the People, but he had no knowledge of other tribes in this area, or whether they were friendly.

While he had traveled alone, it had not been of so much concern. He could change his direction, hide or run easily, and take each day's dangers as they came.

It was different, now. He had assumed responsibility for Yellow Head and her child. There had been no choice. He could not have ridden away to leave them on the prairie. With the responsibility came the necessity to plan, to make wise decisions for the protection of the three travelers. He hoped he would be equal to it.

Tomorrow, he would scout ahead on horseback, then return to walk with Yellow Head while the girl rode the mare. He looked forward to the companionship of someone to share the journey.

Especially, someone as intelligent, courageous, and charming as this attractive woman. He looked across the fire to watch her wrap herself and Sunflower in their robe to sleep. It was a comforting thing, this preparation for the night.

Perhaps, though, he should stand watch. He probably could not sleep anyway.

He rose and made his way to the top of the grassy hill. There, he listened to the night sounds, and watched the Seven Hunters march on their journey. He had just taken on a great deal of new responsibility. Yet there was a certain security in knowing that below the hill slept someone who depended on him for food and protection. It had been a long time since he felt this satisfaction.

He knew it was only temporary, but for now, his heart was good.

30

» » »

The Growers were cooperative, but not much real help. Yellow Head spoke their tongue fairly well, so was able to question them in detail.

"He says he does not know where the Sun Dance was held," she translated. "It is over now, so it is no matter."

"Does he know where the Eastern band will summer?"

"No. They are expected back somewhere in this area within a year."

Such information actually contained nothing that they did not already know.

"Is this the River of Swans?" Cartier asked in sign talk.

"Yes," the Grower nodded. "It comes here from the northwest."

"The river runs north and south at this point," observed Cartier to Yellow Head. "Ask him where its direction from northwest begins."

Yellow Head relayed the question, nodded in answer, and turned again to Cartier.

"He says maybe two, three sleeps."

Cartier thought about it for a moment.

"If the People were camped within three sleeps, these Growers would know," he pondered aloud.

"Yes," Yellow Head agreed.

"And we have come from the southeast. No one we have asked knows where they are."

"Yes."

"Then they must be on the upper part of the river." Yellow Head nodded agreement again.

"Unless they went somewhere else this season," she observed.

"But they have always used this area. Red Feather would not change their territory without reason."

Another possibility came to mind. He turned to the Grower again.

"Is Red Feather still chief?" he signed.

"Yes, of course," the man signed and nodded. "He is a wise chief."

It was some encouragement to learn that these people did actually know those whom they were seeking.

"Let us travel across country northwest," Cartier suggested to Yellow Head, "until we reach the river again. Then we can follow it until we find someone who knows the summer camp."

"Yes," she agreed. "If we do not find them, the Northern band should be somewhere further west."

Cartier nodded, but was not pleased. The woman only wished to reach any of her people. He had reason to find the Eastern band.

Yellow Head saw his face fall.

"I am sorry," she said quickly. "I know you wish to see your son."

Sunflower rode up and slid from the bay mare.

"You need more horses," observed the Grower.

"But we have nothing to trade," signed Cartier.

The man nodded understandingly.

"Still, it is not right for you and your wife to walk while your daughter rides," he persisted.

Sunflower was giggling behind her hand. Cartier looked over at Yellow Head, who was smiling quietly.

"She is not. . . ." he began, then paused. Why try to explain? He changed his unfinished answer.

"She is not riding all of the time. We use the horse for scouting and riding."

He paused, thinking that his statement must have appeared stupid. The Grower seemed not to notice, however. He nodded agreeably.

"Do you have a horse to trade?" asked Cartier.

"No. My brother has. I will show you."

He led the way to a little meadow where a few horses grazed.

"The black one." He pointed.

The animal was of exceptionally good quality, especially considering that the Growers were not noted as horsemen. They may have taken this animal in trade from someone else, thought Cartier. He would have loved to bargain for the black horse, but could not.

"No," he apologized. "I have nothing to trade. Where did your brother get this horse?"

"He raised it. That is the mother."

He pointed to a blue roan mare across the clearing.

The mare had quality about her. Perhaps later, Cartier thought. When he was reestablished as a warrior of the People, he might return to trade. If these Growers had some good stock, this might be a source of new bloodlines.

"I am sorry, my brother," he signed. "Another time, maybe."

He surprised himself a little, that he was slipping back into the ways of the Elk-dog People so rapidly. Here he was, thinking of a horse trade to improve his herd, when he had nothing.

They camped near the Growers' village and moved on the next morning. The three had slipped into a routine that had become comfortable. Cartier would ride ahead and scout the country while the others followed on foot. Then he would return, and allow Sunflower to ride while he and Yellow Head walked and talked. When they neared the end of territory he had scouted, he would ride ahead again.

They would camp for the night at a likely-looking spot with grass for the horse and water available nearby. Their journey was proceeding smoothly. Cartier had even ceased to stand guard at night, beyond a look around from a hilltop just before dusk. After all, they were now in their own country, and he had long since decided that he was not followed.

Therefore, it came as a great surprise when their comfortable routine was interrupted. It was the third evening after they left the Growers, and they were retiring for the night. The stars were scattered, bright as only the velvet blue-black of the prairie sky can make them. Cartier drew his blanket around his shoulders and sat for a moment, watching the fire. Yellow Head was seated on the other side.

Her face was relaxed and calm, and his gaze lingered in appreciation of her beauty. She looked at him and smiled.

Then her gaze shifted, and she was looking beyond and behind him. The large dark eyes widened in terror and she gave a quick little gasp, but did not move. Turning carefully, Cartier looked behind him.

Three warriors stood there in the firelight, weapons at ready. He was certain he had never seen any of them before. He was confused. What did this mean? There was no doubt that their intentions were murderous.

Cartier thought rapidly. Any false move would be his last. Slowly, he raised his right hand in greeting, palm forward.

"Greetings," he signed. "Will you join us, my brothers?"

Behind him, Yellow Head was speaking softly but rapidly in the language of the People.

"They are brothers of the man I killed. I am sorry, Woodchuck. I did not think I was followed."

Now one of the newcomers began to sign.

"We have no bad feeling for you, but the woman is ours."

31

» » »

Cartier sat very still, but glanced quickly around to see how grave this crisis actually was. His bow and arrows were out of reach. It would take an unacceptable amount of time to ready an arrow for a shot, anyway. His light ax lay beside him, and his steel belt knife hung at his waist.

Yellow Head had her flint knife. Sunflower was not in sight. She had apparently gone a little way into the darkness to relieve her bladder before retiring.

The situation appeared grim, against three determined warriors. Two had bows, he noted, and the third carried a short spear. Perhaps he could negotiate, stall for time, until he could think of something.

"The woman is yours?" he signed, assuming a puzzled expression. "How is this?"

"She has killed our brother and fled from us."

"*Aiee!* Surely not! She has not been dangerous since she has been with me. You speak of some other woman."

Moving very deliberately, he began to toss some dry sticks on the fire, causing it to blaze up brightly. He avoided looking directly at the flame, though he hoped the other men would do so. If the afterglow of the fire in their eyes could impair their vision only a little, it might give him an edge.

He turned again to the three figures, using sign talk.

"I will ask my woman of the things you say," he offered.

He spoke in the tongue of the People, for the ears of Yellow Head only. His tone was that of an indignant question, but the words were deliberate.

"Do not look at the fire," he cautioned. "Then our eyes will see better than theirs in the dark."

Yellow Head shook her head in a vigorous denial, meanwhile answering him.

"Yes, it will help."

Now her voice rose as if in argument, loud enough to be heard outside the circle of firelight. To the listeners it appeared that it was a heated argument between the woman and her man, but the content of her words carried different meaning.

"Sunflower!" she shouted in Cartier's face. "Stay where you are! When I tell you, scream your loudest!"

There was silence, but Cartier knew that the girl in the darkness heard and was waiting.

He turned again to the three warriors and began to sign.

"My woman says no. She knows nothing of your brother. My friends, you have the wrong woman."

He smiled amiably, as if the matter was ended. The warriors looked at each other with some doubt in their faces. One moved a little for a better look at Yellow Head.

"No!" he signed irritably. "This is the woman! You have had her only a short while, and do not know her. Now, move aside. We will kill her and let you go."

Cartier felt that he had little choice at this moment. It was time to assert himself.

"Stop! One does not talk of killing another's woman."

The warrior paused uncertainly. One of the others took a step forward.

"You! Stay back," Cartier warned. "My fight is with this dung-eater, who talks of killing women."

Boldly, he picked up his throwing-ax and stood.

"You cannot kill us all," warned the one who seemed to be the leader.

"Then you will be the first to die!" warned Cartier.

He had already decided that the argumentative one was not the target for his ax. The more dangerous foe was the surly one with the spear. He spoke over his shoulder to Yellow Head.

"I will kill the one with the spear and take his weapon. You can pick up my bow and shoot from the darkness."

"Wait," she answered calmly. "I will tell Sunflower to draw their attention."

Her voice rose again, apparently yelling angrily at Cartier.

"Now, Sunflower, now!"

Cartier had heard screams before, but nothing like this. It seemed that the three other men had forgotten the child's existence, so great was their surprise. From directly behind them came a screech that sounded like the legions of the damned. All of the men jumped in alarm. Even Cartier, though he was expecting the sound, had all he could do to keep from recoiling. One of the warriors jumped almost into the fire.

Cartier's throwing-ax was in the air before the scream faded. The man with the spear was flung backward into the darkness, the surprised look on his face destroyed by the impact of the thrown weapon. Cartier was upon him instantly, snatching the short spear and rolling into the darkness. He caught a glimpse of Yellow Head as she snatched his bow and quiver and ran on, dodging across the circle of firelight. An arrow searched after her, into the night, but he did not think it found its mark.

He turned to face the two remaining assailants, gripping his newly acquired spear. They were still within the fire's circle of light, appearing confused at the sudden turn of events. One stared at his fallen comrade in confusion, while the other looked around him in search of a target for the arrow he held ready. He was still looking when an arrow from Yellow Head's bow thudded into the front of his buckskin shirt. The warrior stared at the feathered end of the shaft in disbelief while he sank slowly to the ground.

The other man panicked and ran. Cartier sprinted after him, crouching low. He saw horses ahead, and a figure leaped to the back of the nearest animal Frantically, the man jerked it into a startled leap.

Cartier saw the three horses bolt together to flee, but then pandemonium struck. Without warning, horses were suddenly falling, rolling, plunging, and fighting to keep their feet. The mounted warrior was catapulted high in the air as his horse went down. He landed heavily with a sickening thud, and Cartier was on him in an instant. His assault proved unnecessary. The fallen form was limp.

"Over here," Cartier called. "Bring a torch!"

Yellow Head hurried over, carrying a bundle of blazing sticks.

"He is still alive?" she asked. "Will you kill him?"

"Maybe so. I will take him over to the fire. What happened to the horses?"

The animals were struggling to their feet, plunging nervously. Sunflower came in out of the dark, her eyes bright with excitement.

"I tied them together, and tied the rope around that tree," she said simply.

Even in the stress of the moment, Cartier had to laugh. He had not been able to understand the animals' strange behavior.

"You did well, little one."

They dragged the unconscious form to the light of the fire, and examined him for injuries. Beyond a massive lump above the left ear and assorted scrapes and scratches, there seemed to be no wounds. The man was beginning to stir.

Cartier could not bring himself to kill a helpless prisoner. He brought a thong and tied his hands and feet.

"We will release him in the morning."

Some time later, Cartier and Yellow Head sat watching the flames, this time on the same side of the fire. Across from them, Sunflower slept the exhausted sleep of childhood on her mother's robe. The prisoner lay fettered at the edge of the lighted circle.

Excitement still ran high in the two by the fire. There was no question of sleep yet. For a while they sat in silence, each reliving the rapid events of the evening. It had all happened so suddenly.

It was Yellow Head who finally broke the silence.

"I am sorry, Woodchuck, to bring danger to you."

"It is nothing. You did not know."

She stared at the fire a little longer.

"I did not think you would fight. You are a good man, Woodchuck."

Cartier smiled, embarrassed.

"There was little choice."

"You called me your woman."

"The others thought it so. There was no time to explain." He was stumbling a little over the words. "It seemed better," he finished lamely.

They sat in silence for a little while. Yellow Head turned to look at him for a moment, as if she had not really seen him before. Her eyes were large and dark in the firelight.

"But you fought for me," she said softly.

32
» » »

The next morning, Cartier evaluated the three horses of their enemy. He chose the two best to keep, as well as assorted weapons for Yellow Head and Sunflower. Then he went to the prisoner and cut the thongs that bound his wrists and ankles behind him. Painfully, the young man struggled to a sitting position.

"How are you called?" Cartier asked the question in sign talk.

"I am Black Squirrel. You will kill me now?"

"No. We give back your weapons."

"And then kill me?"

"No. We give you a horse, too. Go home, tell your tribe that they are not to steal women of the Elk-dog People."

He pointed to the two bodies that he had dragged from the camp.

"This is how our People handle stealers of women."

The young man nodded.

"I will tell them. And how are you called?"

A hint of warning sounded, far in the dim recesses of Cartier's mind. This young warrior was too cooperative. Perhaps they should have killed him, after all.

"I am Woodchuck, of the Southern band."

If the warrior meant vengeance, there was no way to prevent his learning their identity. He might as well know from the start.

Yellow Head led a horse to the prisoner and handed the rein.

"This is not my horse," the young man signed. "The other one, the gray."

"No," Cartier answered quickly. "This is your horse, now. We keep the others."

He handed the warrior a bow and two arrows, and a small flint knife.

"This will let you kill food."

A dark look flickered for a moment across the face of Black Squirrel. Or could it have been only Cartier's imagination? The young warrior nodded his appreciation.

"I will do as you say," he promised.

There was still something ingratiating about the man's too-ready cooperation, thought Cartier. Could he be planning vengeance? Ah well, no matter. They would soon be far away.

Yellow Head was finishing their preparations for travel. It would be much faster and easier now, with three horses. Sunflower was delighted with the spotted mare Cartier chose for her.

"She is mine, Woodchuck?"

"Of course."

"To keep?"

"Yes, little one," he chuckled. "She will be yours for many summers."

For most of the day, Cartier would scout ahead and then watch the back trail. He must make certain that they were not followed by the defeated warrior, Black Squirrel. He spent most of the night on watch, but saw no sign that anything was amiss.

They rose with the sun and moved on. The conformation of the land gave indication that they might be approaching the river again. They had cut across open country to save traveling distance, and reach the area where the People were expected.

Cartier had just rejoined the others after another careful scout on the back trail when Yellow Head startled him with a question.

"Do you see the man on the hill ahead?"

He reined in quickly.

"No, do not stop. Keep moving as we were," she cautioned.

"Who is it? Our prisoner?"

"I think not, Woodchuck."

Cartier studied the figure, trying not to appear to do so. The man sat on his horse on the crest of a low hill to the southwest. It was obvious that he was watching them. It was also obvious that he wished to be seen. This was deliberate, the appearance on the hill, an announcement of his presence.

"He does not behave like an enemy," Yellow Head observed.

Cartier agreed.

"Unless, of course, there is a large war party behind the hill."

"I think not, Woodchuck. They would stay hidden and surprise us. I think maybe he is one of our wolves."

"Wolves" were scouts or outriders used when the People were traveling, Cartier had learned long ago. The term apparently referred to the manner in which a few wolves always seemed to circle the edges of a moving buffalo herd.

"Ours? The People?"

"Maybe so. We will see."

Cartier was confused by her nonchalance.

"Should we ride that way?"

"There is no need. Our paths will cross, ahead. Then we will see."

"Could this be an enemy tribe on the move?"

"No. There are none here in strength. And this is a

large party, to show their wolves so boldly. It must be the People."

Her matter-of-fact logic was so reasonable that Cartier wondered why he had not been able to arrive at the same conclusions.

Now the watcher on the hill was joined by two others. Together, the three riders moved out at a leisurely lope, directly toward Cartier's little party. He could not avoid the uneasy prickle of his neck hairs and the sweating of his palms. He glanced at Yellow Head, who gave him a nervous smile.

"I think they are ours, Woodchuck. But I will be ready."

The three newcomers were now pounding across a level stretch of plain, two or three bow-shots away. Cartier reined in his bay, and turned to face the approaching warriors. He sat loosely, trying to appear confident and at ease. As they approached, he raised his right hand, palm open, in greeting.

"They are ours!" Yellow Head said softly. "Look at their moccasins!"

It was true. The pattern of the riders' footwear was unmistakably that of the People.

The riders came to a sliding stop a few steps away, their horses' hooves scattering dust and small chunks of sod. Three grim faces glared at Cartier.

"Who are you?" the leader demanded in sign talk. "What is your tribe?"

"The People, the Elk-dog People," the astonished Cartier blurted.

"No!" retorted the other. "You speak our tongue, but I do not know you."

"We are of the Southern band."

"But none of you wears the garments of the People." The man pointed in derision.

Cartier looked at his companions, who were wearing the dress of the tribe who had been their captors. As for himself, his buckskins were those of the faraway Big

Lakes country. His beard, also, belied his claim. The explanation would be long and complicated. He heaved a deep sigh.

"My friends," he began, "my name is Woodchuck. I . . ."

"Stupid ones," Yellow Head interrupted, scolding. "This man married the daughter of Red Feather. Do you want your chief to know how you received his family?"

The three warriors looked at each other uneasily.

"You are Woodchuck?" one asked, still unsure.

"Of course! My son, who lives in the lodge of the chief, is called Ground Squirrel. Or, he was, when I left."

"He is called Red Feather, now, since his naming ceremony," added Yellow Head. "His grandfather gave him his own name."

"That is true," one man admitted. "Who are you, woman?"

"Yellow Head, of the Southern band. We were stolen, and my husband killed, three summers past."

"Ah yes. His name was Yellow Horse."

"*Aiee!* Do not speak the name of the dead!" she cried in alarm.

"It is all right. Someone gave a child his name. Yes, I remember now. We heard that most of two families were killed."

"That is true. Only now could we come home."

Puzzled, the man looked from her to Cartier.

"You have been a prisoner, too, Woodchuck?"

"No," Cartier mumbled, perhaps more embarrassed than was appropriate. "We met on the prairie as we traveled."

The other man looked from Cartier to the woman and back again. It was obvious that he had assumed them to be man and wife.

"Oh. I . . . it is no matter. Look, the People come."

He pointed to the crest of the hill. Straggling into sight came the first of the families. Baggage and lodge covers

144

were piled high on pole-drags behind the horses. Dogs and children ran alongside.

Cartier watched them a moment, then turned to Yellow Head with a smile. They had found the People.

33

» » »

They rode to the main group with the three wolves, who were calling out the news. There was a great deal of interest in the stories of the former prisoner, Yellow Head, and Woodchuck, who had not been seen for five seasons. Still, it was necessary to keep moving. The site for the summer camp should be reached today.

Cartier managed to free himself from questioning well-wishers. He must find Red Feather's family and his son. Yellow Head spoke to him aside.

"Woodchuck, we will go with you to pay respects to the chief, but then we will stay with my aunt. I thank you for your help."

She gave him the wonderful smile that he had come to prize so highly. They had been through much together, and he already felt a sense of loss. She had not mentioned until now that she had relatives here, but he knew that most of the People were related to those in other bands. Somehow, he had envisioned the three of them as guests in the lodge of Red Feather. Even as he thought this, he realized that he had come to think of the three as a family unit.

"You will stay with your aunt until the Big Council next season?"

He knew her desire to return to her own, the Southern band.

"Maybe so. I will ask where the Southern band is summering."

So, he thought, she was considering traveling to her own band. This concerned him for her safety and that of Sunflower, but he said nothing. He had no right to question her plans, which actually had not even been stated yet.

"Woodchuck!" someone shouted.

Red Feather loped forward and leaned from his horse to embrace his son-in-law.

"They said you were here! I hoped it was true, but did not really believe it!"

"It is true, Uncle," Cartier assured him, using the customary term of respect among the People. "It is good to be back. Is Crow Wing well, and my son?"

"Yes, yes. They will take joy in your coming."

He paused and looked briefly at Yellow Head and Sunflower.

"This is your woman and child?"

"No, Uncle. I found them on the prairie. Yellow Head is of the Southern band. They were stolen, three summers ago."

"Ah yes, I remember. We heard of it."

He turned to Yellow Head.

"You are welcome in my lodge, daughter, until you can return to your own."

"Thank you, my chief, but we will stay with my aunt."

"It is good. But if you need help, my lodge is yours."

The young woman murmured her thanks.

"Woodchuck," she added, "we will go to find my aunt now."

He watched the two ride on, and his heart was heavy. Somehow he was not prepared for this separation. It was ridiculous, he told himself irritably. He would see them nearly every day.

"Come," Red Feather was saying. "You will wish to see your son."

"He is a good son?" Cartier asked, immediately realizing that it was a ridiculous question to ask a grandfather.

"Yes, he learns well. He is a thinker, that one." The chief chuckled.

Yes, thought Cartier, and he would be taught well by Red Feather.

The meeting was a little clumsy, the boy embarrassed and Cartier not knowing quite what to say. However, the warm reception by Red Feather and Crow Wing quickly melted any reservations on the part of anyone. Young Red Feather, still called by the pet name of Ground Squirrel to avoid confusion with his grandfather's name, soon warmed to the father he did not remember.

"He looks much like Cloud," Cartier commented, misty-eyed.

"Yes, that is our joy, too," answered Crow Wing.

There was much to be done, and Cartier made himself useful in the heavy work of erecting the lodgepoles and lifting the cover.

"*Aiee*, it is good to have an extra pair of arms," observed Crow Wing.

"Yes, my son, it is good to have you back," said Red Feather seriously. "Come, the lodge is up. Let us smoke."

They walked a little way from the new camp, and sat watching the activity below. Red Feather filled two pipes and handed them to Cartier while he kindled a flame with rubbing-sticks and a fire-bow.

He handed a blazing tinder to his guest and lighted his own pipe also. Both pipes were soon producing puffs of fragrant white smoke, and the two men relaxed.

"*Aiee*," observed Red Feather. "It is better when one may light a pipe from the coals of the cooking fire."

He stowed his fire-sticks in their pouch and laid it aside. They smoked a long time in silence.

"Tell me, my son, has it been good with you?"

"Yes, Uncle," he lied.

How could he tell of the bleak despair, the hopelessness of his bereavement?

"My heart has been very heavy for Pink Cloud, but it is better now."

"The woman, Yellow Head?"

"No, Uncle. I was better even before I met her. I had to learn to mourn."

Red Feather nodded understandingly.

"It is a hard thing, sometimes. But tell me, my son, about this woman. She is not really yours?"

"No. I met them on the trail. She told me her story, and we traveled together. We had to kill two men who followed her."

"Why?"

"She killed the man who held her as his wife. His brothers followed her and wished to take her. I killed one, she another, and a third we captured and then released."

"*Aiee!* This is a strong woman. You are fortunate to find her!"

Without waiting for comment on that odd statement, Red Feather continued.

"But it may be a mistake, Woodchuck, to let the one man go."

"I think not, Uncle. He has not followed us. But what did you mean about the woman?"

Red Feather chuckled.

"It is plain in the way you look at each other. *Aiee,* Woodchuck, I could not believe she is not your woman. She wishes it so."

Cartier was confused. Then why had Yellow Head brushed him aside as soon as they reached the People, to go to her aunt's lodge?

Then he remembered the quiet conversation in the night, after the three warriors had been defeated. Yes, she had had feelings for him, and he had denied any such thoughts. He remembered her quiet comment: "But you fought for me."

How could he have been such an idiot?

Red Feather was voicing similar sentiments.

"You must talk to her, Woodchuck. It is not often that one finds such a woman. Does she have a father and mother?"

"I do not know, Uncle. I must find out."

"Yes, you must."

"But now, tell me. You have seen Sky-Eyes and Pale Star? They are well, no? And their children?"

"Ah yes," smiled Red Feather. "They have a girl and a smaller boy. You knew that?"

"Yes, Yellow Head told me, but she has been gone three summers."

"Yes. They are respected. Sky-Eyes is as important a subchief as an outsider could be."

Yes, thought Cartier, that is as I would expect. These were two people who had been an important part of his life, had shared his joys and grief, and had cared for his infant son after Cloud's death. He longed to see them.

Ground Squirrel was coming up the slope toward them.

"The meat is ready," he called.

The two men rose and, on each side of the spirited youngster, made their way to the lodge for the evening meal.

34

» » »

During the long days of summer, Woodchuck became acquainted with his son. Children had always been attracted to him, and young Ground Squirrel was no exception.

Sometimes they rode, the youngster proudly riding the horse that his grandfather had given him. Woodchuck took a great deal of pride in his son's skill. He could tell that the boy felt the same affinity for the prairie, the tallgrass country, that he himself had found only as a grown man.

Sometimes they were joined by Sunflower, who assumed the motherly role of an older sister to the boy. She could change in an instant from a playful, giggling child to a nurturing adult, gently instructing, helping, reprimanding. Ground Squirrel immediately began to relate to the girl, aided by the fact that both held Woodchuck almost in awe.

Sometimes other children were included in their pastimes. The children who remembered Woodchuck from his previous stay with the People were now somewhat older, and were assuming the duties and pursuits of adults. Young warriors and their wives spoke pleasantly to him. In most cases he did not specifically remember them as children, but was pleased at their reactions. Again, he was kept busy carving small wooden objects which he gave to the children who followed them. More boys would reach manhood treasuring a small fetish carved by Woodchuck. More warriors in their later years would proudly display these medicine-objects, and proudly recount the circumstances of their association with Woodchuck.

Perhaps for him, however, the best times of all were those spent alone with his son. They walked through the prairie and along the streams, sharing the sights, sounds, and smells. They saw fat tadpoles in the puddles of the creek, and discussed how they could become giant frogs in another year. Woodchuck insisted that such things were eaten in his country, but Ground Squirrel did not believe him. In the deeper holes they could watch the silvery flash of minnows as they darted to escape the predatory approach of larger fish.

Together, they marveled at the way the red-tailed hawks could circle for long periods of time without moving their wings. Even more so, the buzzards, who seemed never to move their wings at all.

They watched the scattered bands of elk, antelope, and buffalo that grazed on the lush grass of the prairie. It was not yet the season of the fall hunts, and only enough hunting for current use was being done. Therefore, the animals remained relatively undisturbed. They saw the immediate reaction in defense of a buffalo calf who gave a bleating cry for help when threatened by a young gray wolf. Almost instantly, the entire band of cows rushed to the aid of the youngster. The front they presented, of lowered heads and tossing horns, effectively discouraged the young wolf, who decided rapidly that discretion was the wisdom of the day. Ground Squirrel chuckled in amusement.

"You will stay with the People, now?" the youngster asked seriously one day.

"Yes, I will stay."

"It is good," said the boy simply, walking with his hand in that of his father.

Crow Wing watched the growing closeness between the two.

"The boy grows away from us," she observed with sadness.

"No," replied Red Feather. "He will still have us. Now he has his father, too. That is good, for him to know his father. It is as it should be. I am glad Woodchuck has come back."

Increasingly, Cartier thought of himself as Woodchuck. He was accepted by the People as one of their own who had now returned. It was easy to fall back into the life-style that had been such a part of him with Pink Cloud. He smoked and talked with the other men, sometimes hunted with them when fresh meat was needed. He seldom thought of himself now as Sergeant Jean Cartier. That part of his past drew further and further behind him. Each day, he became more completely Woodchuck, warrior and hunter of the People.

He saw Yellow Head only infrequently. On these occasions, both were uncomfortable. It seemed that there was much to say, yet they had great difficulty in approaching it. Instead, they discussed the weather, the children, anything that seemed to avoid any thought or feeling.

Woodchuck, as always, was impressed by her beauty on these occasions. Her large, deep-set eyes seemed like dark pools of mystery. Her features, soft yet strong, were changeable with her moods. He found himself admiring the way she moved, the swing of her hips as she walked, and the curve of her legs below the fringe of her buckskin dress. The entire impression was that of willowy grace. Yet he knew from experience that she could be tough as rawhide.

Somehow, he never quite got around to asking her about her parents. It was nothing conscious on his part. It was simply that in her presence, he was preoccupied. Only later would he remember.

One afternoon, as he was grooming the bay mare, she approached him self-consciously. Ground Squirrel had gone off somewhere with Sunflower, so they were quite alone.

"Woodchuck," she began, "Sunflower and I are leaving tomorrow."

He straightened and looked at her in astonishment.

"Leaving?"

"Yes. The Southern band is camped on Cedar River. I can find them in nine, ten sleeps."

"But alone?"

"Of course." Her voice was crisp. "We were alone before we found you!"

And alone again, he finished the unspoken accusation to himself.

"But, Yellow Head, I . . ."

There was so much he wanted to say, and he was having so much difficulty.

"I will live in my parents' lodge." She answered his unasked question. "My aunt says they are well, but they think I am dead."

"Yes, you should go to them," he said slowly, "but you should not go alone. I will go with you."

"No!" she snapped. "Your place is here. I do not need you!"

"But I wish to see Sky-Eyes and Pale Star. I had thought of going, anyway."

Somehow, this was not going well at all. Perhaps, he thought, I am trying to avoid the main problem. Perhaps Red Feather was right: "She is not your woman? She wishes it so."

And I wish it so, he admitted. Now, because of his caution, and the old hurt of his previous loss, he was about to lose her, too.

"Yellow Head," he said slowly, "I had hoped we might share a lodge, you and I."

She turned her back to him and stood as if staring at the far horizon. The heartbeats ticked away the time for a few moments, while Woodchuck stood helpless. This must be difficult for her, too, he realized.

Finally she turned to face him again. Her eyes were moist, and the soft sad smile flickered across her lips.

"It is good, Woodchuck," she almost whispered.

35

》 》 》

They were married in the simple ceremony of the People, before they started the journey. Red Feather took the part of the girl's father, and spread the robe around their shoulders as they stood together, signifying that they were one.

There was much feasting that night, and well-wishing by a myriad of people, before the two retired to themselves in a quiet glade some distance from the camp. The soft song of the creek over the sandy shallows made a pleasant murmur. A coyote called in the distance, and another answered. The shared warmth of their bodies seemed fitting on a cool prairie night, their first together on a shared sleeping robe.

Sunflower, approaching the age of romantic fantasy, had been thrilled by this turn of events. Ground Squirrel, not yet quite secure in the return of his father, still thought the acquisition of a sister an exciting prospect.

Woodchuck and Yellow Head had discussed the matter of the children at some length. Both felt that to uproot Ground Squirrel from the only home he had known would be unwise, in so sudden a change. They talked with Red Feather and Crow Wing.

They were sitting in front of the chief's lodge, watch-

ing the children at play. Sunflower was showing the boy
how to roll a cottonwood leaf to make a toy lodge, complete with smoke flaps. They had constructed a whole
encampment of leaf-lodges, and were happily pretending
some children's game in their toy village.

"You could leave Sunflower here," offered Crow Wing.
"She would be a big help to us, and is so good with
Ground Squirrel."

It was not unusual, Woodchuck recalled, to leave children with a relative for a season. The entire tribe assem-
bled yearly, and there was frequent communication and
travel during the rest of the year.

"Yes!" exclaimed Red Feather. "Then at the Big Council, you can take them both if you wish."

The plan sounded good. It would give Sunflower the
alternative of Red Feather's lodge or visiting her aunt.
Ground Squirrel could have the continuity of relating to
his new sister. Meanwhile, Woodchuck and Yellow Head
would establish their lodge, with the expectation of
regaining both children in a few moons' time.

The children were delighted, though Ground Squirrel
voiced slight doubts.

"You will come back?"

"Of course. We will meet at the Big Council, next
Moon of Roses. You will be with Red Feather and Crow
Wing, and Sunflower will stay with you."

Ground Squirrel thought a moment, then broke into a
broad grin.

"It is good!"

One extra advantage of the plan was that it furnished
the lovers uninterrupted time together while they traveled. There was no hurry, so theirs was a leisurely pace,
with many chances to talk, to enjoy each other's company, and to spend time snuggled in the sleeping robes.

Once a summer storm threatened, and they took refuge
under the overhang of a nearby bluff. Rain Maker's drum
rumbled and his spears of real-fire crashed to earth as the
advancing storm front swept across the grassland. Then

the prairie was obscured by the colorless gray nothingness and the rain descended in torrents.

The storm was short-lived, however. In a little while it had passed, and the creatures of the prairie came forth again. Birds sang what appeared to be songs of joy for the sunshine, which returned to sparkle for a little while on clean-washed grass before night descended. They were able to see a spectacular rainbow across the eastern sky just before dark.

"Sun Boy paints in beautiful colors tonight," observed Yellow Head.

"Never better," agreed Woodchuck.

He gently placed his arm around her shoulders, and she responded by slipping hers around his waist. She leaned her head against him.

"It gives me much happiness that we happened to meet on the trail," she said solemnly.

"Yes," he agreed. "It is good that we did not kill each other."

Both laughed, but both knew it could have happened. It had been a very dangerous meeting.

"Then it is good that I called you what I did?" she teased.

"Of course. That was how I knew you were of the People."

"*Aiee*, but to have my first words to you be obscene!"

"It is nothing. You have said many good things to me since then."

They laughed again. They were becoming more comfortable together.

"Come, let us make camp," Yellow Head suggested. "It is too late to travel, and too wet to make camp in the dark."

In the end, they camped under the shelter of the bluff, and watched the moon rise, full and bloodred above the receding bank of storm clouds at the distant horizon.

Next morning they rose and traveled again. Travel was good, the rain having softened the earth, but drained and dried enough to eliminate slippery footing. The prairie slipped behind them.

"Do you know where we are going?" he asked.

"I think so. There is a favorite spot on Cedar River. Sometimes we even winter there."

"How far?"

"Maybe two sleeps now." She chuckled, the delightful sound that he loved. "Three, if we camp longer."

She was beginning to recall landmarks, and suggested that they stay out the extra day, to avoid hurried travel and late arrival. Both knew that these were excuses. Both wanted more time together, before resuming the responsibilities of tribal life.

Finally came the day when their almost idyllic journey would end. They rose, extinguished the fire, and packed their few belongings on the horses.

"We should reach the village by midday," Yellow Head informed him.

They were quiet as they rode this morning. It was plain that both were reluctant to complete the journey. Almost with disappointment, they reined in at the top of a ridge to look for the expected camp site.

Yes, there it was in the distance. The familiar blur of gray-white smoke from cooking fires hung over a distant valley.

"There." Yellow Head pointed.

"Yes."

They started down the slope.

"Your parents think you dead?" Woodchuck asked.

"Yes, so my aunt said. They thought I would never stay a prisoner."

"You did not. My friends think me dead, too."

This could become a problem. Where should they go first? There were many explanations which they must make.

"Let us separate when we reach the camp," suggested Yellow Head. "We can each tell our stories, and then come back together."

That seemed the simplest course of action. They touched heels to their horses and approached the camp at a gentle lope. Now that they were this close, both were looking eagerly ahead to their reunions.

36

Cartier threaded his way among the lodges.

"*Aiee*, Woodchuck!" someone called in greeting.

"*Ah-koh*, brother," he returned. "Could you tell me where is the lodge of Sky-Eyes and Pale Star?"

"Right over there." The man pointed. "It is good to see you back, Woodchuck."

"It is good to be back," he answered, turning his horse in the indicated direction.

A man was reclining against a willow backrest in front of one of the lodges. Cartier nearly passed him by. He did not have any preconceived notion as to how his former commanding officer might look, but somehow this warrior did not fit the picture. This man's hair was plaited in the manner of the People, he wore well-used buckskins, and his facial hair was cleanly plucked.

As the rider passed, the man half rose. Cartier paused for another look. The shade of the sky-blue eyes betrayed the warrior's identity. Cartier reined to a stop.

"Lieutenant Du Pres?"

"*Mon dieu!* Cartier?"

Du Pres leaped to his feet.

The rider dismounted, and the two embraced briefly.

Both started to talk at once, paused to laugh, and both talked again.

"You first," suggested Du Pres in French.

"Very well, Lieutenant." He paused a moment. "Well, I have returned."

"Yes . . . go on."

Cartier shrugged.

"I stopped at the lodge of Red Feather and Crow Wing, and saw my son. He is a wonderful child, Lieutenant."

"Yes," agreed Du Pres, "but . . ."

The door-flap of the lodge opened, and Pale Star looked out.

"*Aiee!*" she exclaimed in delight. "Woodchuck! You have returned. You will stay with us?"

A small boy with large gray-green eyes peered from around the lodge.

"Your son?" asked Cartier.

"Yes. Have you seen our daughter?"

"No."

"Wait!" Du Pres was insistent. "Tell me of your trip."

"I met a woman, called Yellow Head. You will like her, Star. We were married when we stopped with the Eastern band."

Pale Star was like a little girl in her delight.

"Where is she, Woodchuck?"

"She stopped at her parents' lodge. Maybe you will remember her. She was the wife of Yellow Horse."

"Ah yes. I know her well. She is my friend. It is good, Woodchuck."

"Sergeant!" Du Pres all but shouted.

The other two turned to him in astonishment.

"I want your report," he demanded icily, in crisp, military French.

"Yes, Lieutenant."

Unconsciously, Cartier assumed a position at military attention.

"First, where are the others?"

"Others, sir?" Cartier was mystified.

"Yes, the expedition?"

"Expedition? They were going down the Big River. I left them and came overland."

He was puzzled. How did the lieutenant know about an expedition?

"They were not coming here?" Du Pres persisted. "You are not guiding them back?"

"No sir."

Cartier began to understand. If he had delivered the lieutenant's journal, there might have been a thrust to colonize immediately. He had not only destroyed the packet, he had falsified its contents.

"Did you deliver the journal?"

"No sir. I lost it on the trip to Mishi-ghan."

"You *lost* it?"

"It was destroyed in a fire, sir."

This was becoming very uncomfortable.

"What did you report?"

"That the West was desert, not worth colonizing, sir."

"But why? It is excellent country."

"I did not want the People to become like the natives there, sir," his voice was pleading, "killing each other for the bounties paid for scalps. It would not be fitting for the Elk-dog People."

"But you led an expedition back downriver!"

"Yes sir, but not here. They wanted to find the southern sea."

"And you left them?"

"Yes. I came home."

His action had seemed much more logical at the time. Du Pres bristled with anger.

"Sergeant," he said coldly, "you have lost a military report, falsified its contents, and now, deserted your unit. *Mon dieu*, you are guilty of treason!"

Cartier had expected almost any reception except this. In his eagerness to return to the People, he had almost overlooked the fact that he might have to explain his actions to Du Pres.

163

Pale Star stood, watching and listening intently. She started to speak, then seemed to realize that it was up to Cartier to reply.

The sergeant stood, embarrassed and confused. He was being accused unjustly, he felt. In truth, he felt that he was the one who was betrayed. He drew himself up to full height and dignity.

"Lieutenant," he said formally, "part of what you say is true. I failed to deliver the report, and I misled Captain Le Blanc as to its contents. This I did for the good of my family and yours. It is true that I left the expedition, but they are in capable hands. I have done nothing to bring danger or dishonor to my country or the Crown."

He paused, nervous and sweating. This was a long speech for him. Du Pres started to speak, but Cartier waved him down.

"You have accused me of treason, Lieutenant. This is a serious charge. I am no more guilty of desertion or treason than you, Lieutenant. You have been out here with your family for five years, without attempting to report to your commander. They think you dead!"

Du Pres was furious. He was standing almost toe-to-toe with the sergeant, and seemed to be at a loss for his next move.

"Now you have defied the authority of a superior officer."

Du Pres fairly sputtered in his anger. He glanced around. Near his right shoulder hung his rawhide shield, on its pole in front of the lodge. With it were his weapons. His hand reached out.

Cartier thought for a moment that the lieutenant reached for his lance, but that was not his purpose. Du Pres seized a quirt that hung there and swung it at the sergeant's face. The lash bit across his cheek and upper lip like a burning coal, and Cartier felt the trickle of blood, salty to his lips. Still at attention, he did not move.

"Sergeant, you are under arrest!"

"And what then, sir? You will have to take me back, or kill me here."

He turned on his heel, deliberately exposing his back to the lieutenant. He was only moderately confident that Du Pres would not strike him in the back. He picked up the rein of the bay mare and swung to her back. Seldom had he felt more depressed and disappointed. Truly, his world had turned to ashes, and it had been a complete surprise. Only with great difficulty could he bring himself to speak. He reined the mare around to face Du Pres.

"Lieutenant," he managed to say, his throat tight with emotion, "you cannot have it both ways."

He turned the bay mare to ride away.

"Woodchuck! Wait!" Pale Star called after him.

He spoke over his shoulder, barely pausing.

"It is all right, Star. I will stay with my wife's people."

37
» » »

The People were puzzled over the strange behavior of Sky-Eyes and Woodchuck. These two friends of long standing were now angry and bitter at each other, and the People did not know why. Both men were well-liked and respected, and the hearts of the People were heavy over their strange behavior.

Somehow, it appeared that Sky-Eyes thought Woodchuck should not have returned. Or, it seemed to some, that he thought Woodchuck should have returned sooner. Again, Woodchuck seemed to resent the fact that Sky-Eyes had *not* returned to their own tribe. The whole thing was very confusing, and there was regret that the two seemed unable to settle their differences.

Probably the one who had the greatest understanding of the entire problem was Pale Star. She had spent several years among the French in Mishi-ghan, and had observed the strange customs of the military hierarchy. She knew that her husband had had authority over Woodchuck, but had assumed that it was in the past. Among the People, there was not the rigid chain of command. Besides, authority had a tendency to wax and wane with the political popularity of each leader. A chieftain whose band fell on bad times might see several families join other bands for a season or two. Or, conversely, the band of a highly successful leader, whose medicine was strong, might grow in size.

She wondered if Woodchuck might join the Eastern band over this disagreement, whatever it was. She hoped not. The two men needed each other. During the year that the two couples had shared a lodge, she had seen the strength that they found from their friendship. Now, even the friendship was gone, and for reasons that were a mystery.

"It has to do with customs of their tribe." Star tried to explain to her friend Yellow Head.

"But I do not understand. They are not with their tribe now. Both are men of the People."

"Yes, but as you know yourself, one never completely escapes who he is."

"That is true. Do you know why they disagree?"

Star gave a discouraged sigh.

"I heard the argument. Each thinks the other has broken the laws of their tribe, the *Fran-coy.*"

"Did they?"

Star smiled sadly.

"Probably. One, no more than the other. Their customs are strange. They do not change bands as we do. They have a real-chief who is called King Louis, far across the salty Big Water. They must obey him."

"*Aiee!* How can he be a good chief from across the Big Water?"

"I have wondered. You must ask them . . . no, best not to ask them anything about it for now."

Both women giggled, though there was more hurt than humor here.

"We must do what we can to make peace between them, Star," Yellow Head observed seriously.

"Yes. We will think about it. I will talk to your husband, if I may?"

"Of course. Come over to our lodge."

Woodchuck and Yellow Head were planning for their

own lodge, but for the present were still with her parents. The two women walked there to find Woodchuck. He was gloomy and morose.

"*Ah-koh*, Woodchuck," greeted Star.

"*Ah-koh*, Star."

"Woodchuck, I wish to help. What can be done to restore peace between you and my husband?"

"Nothing, I think. Sky-Eyes says I have betrayed my own people."

"Yes, I know."

"Do you think so?" he pleaded.

"It does not seem so to me. No more than my husband, anyway."

"But he will not talk to me."

"You cannot solve your differences without talking."

"I know this. Star, can you talk to Sky-Eyes? Maybe you can find out how to fix this."

"I will try, Woodchuck. Tell me, he thinks you disobeyed your orders?"

"Yes. Maybe I did. But his orders were to report back, and he is still here. Maybe we should both go back to Mishi-ghan."

"No, no," said Star quickly. "That would admit that you are both wrong!"

She had no desire to return to the land of perennial conflict between French and Yen-glees.

"Would it not be better to feel that you are both *right?*" she suggested.

"But how can that be? Sky-Eyes has accused me of treason."

He used the French term, not knowing whether the People even had a word for "treason."

"I know. I heard. You also accused Sky-Eyes."

"Yes." Woodchuck was troubled.

"Look, Woodchuck. Your reasons for what you have both done are the same. You wish to be with your families. That is not a bad thing."

"Maybe not."

"So, you must feel that both have done right."

"Yes, I have thought so, Star. I think so, yet."

"Then you think it is right for Sky-Eyes to have stayed here?"

"Of course. That is why I came back. Can you talk to him of this?"

"I will try, but I do not know, Woodchuck."

Her attempt to make peace between the two met with immovable opposition. Sky-Eyes not only refused to talk about it, but forbade her to talk to Woodchuck again. That proved to be an error of judgment on his part. Pale Star drew herself up to her full height and stared at him regally. The dark eyes flashed fire.

"I will talk to my friends if I please, Sky-Eyes. Now, listen. You are both wrong, and both right. You must talk together, and decide what you must do. I will help if I can, but do not tell me who I must or must not talk to!"

He watched her retreating figure, her indignation showing in every muscle as she walked. This was one of the things that had attracted him originally. Intelligence, backed up by self-confidence.

"Star, wait!"

He hurried after her.

"Star, I am made to feel that you are right. I must talk with Woodchuck. Will you tell him this?"

"Of course."

"Now, Woodchuck and I should be alone, no?"

"Yes, I think so."

"Then tell him. I will meet him, on that hilltop." He pointed. "We will talk."

The hill was some distance from camp, farther than someone might walk under usual circumstances. It was one of the flat-topped hills of the tallgrass prairie, commanding a view in all directions. It would be a good place to talk.

"It is good," Star said approvingly. "When?"

He thought a moment.

"Sunset. Just before Sun Boy goes to the other side."

Star smiled. She was pleased. Both men, she knew, had reveled in the glory of the prairie sunsets. It would be difficult to maintain the stubborn streak that now afflicted them both, in the face of such beauty.

"It is good!" she nodded. "I will tell him."

be suited. Buy was pleased. He was sure. She knew had relied an exceedingly for the place. Know no. It would b almost to stand the stat[?] give new al

38
» » »

Du Pres sat at the rim of the hill, waiting. His horse was cropping grass a little distance away, and the sun was low in the west. He was watching, waiting for Cartier.

He was glad that Pale Star had intervened in their quarrel. It removed some of the responsibility for the deterioration of their friendship, and at least would allow them to save face.

Gradually, he had come to realize that he and Cartier shared the same dilemma. Their choice was between this life, with the People, or return to the regimented confusion of life in the frontier garrisons. After much thought, he had become ready to admit that in part, Sergeant Cartier was right. There had been a period of five years in which, had he really wished, he could have returned to his military duties at any time. He had managed to convince himself that he was waiting for an expedition that would come as a result of his journal, carried back by Cartier. He realized now that this had been an unrealistic expectation. There was even an uneasy feeling that he had actually dreaded the changes that an expedition would bring about.

All his doubts and feelings of guilt had rushed to the surface with the unexpected reappearance of Cartier. Du

Pres had not yet fully admitted, but had begun to see what he had done. He had quickly attempted to blame Cartier for his own shortcomings.

And, just as quickly, the fat was in the fire. He, Du Pres, could not back down from the official position he had taken. Just as surely, Cartier was unable to retract his words, which had made him guilty of insubordination at the least. At worst, the sergeant was guilty of treason.

Aiee, Du Pres thought, how to resolve this? They must discuss it calmly, as friends with a mutual problem. He thought this could be done.

There seemed to be two courses of action. On either one, both of them must agree completely.

They could return together to report to Fort Mishighan, with a story as near the truth as possible, sparing possible guilt on the part of either man. Cartier could say, for instance, that he had become separated from the exploring party, had encountered Du Pres, whom he had believed dead, and brought him back.

Du Pres, on the other hand, could imply that he had been prevented from returning by the natives, until now. There were flaws in the story, but it could be made to work.

The problem that he saw with this solution was that of their families. He did not think that either of them could leave their families here. That presented the problem of traveling across the continent with their wives and four children. It could be done, of course, but would require complete cooperation on the part of the women. Somehow, he hesitated to mention such a thing to Pale Star. He knew her well, and feared that she might simply refuse to leave her people again.

He had reached an impasse with this possibility, at least until he could talk with Cartier.

The other major alternative that came to mind at first seemed completely impossible. They could simply remain with the People. When Cartier had returned and accused him of being remiss in his loyalty, he had been enraged. Gradually, he realized that he had accused Cartier first. When the entire course of events for the last few years was viewed realistically, they were equally guilty, and of the same crime. Both were avoiding return to the complications of the civilized world. Both had found the stark hardness of the nomadic life honest and realistic. It was not easy, but the goals and rewards were plain to see.

The tragedies, also, he realized. They had seen friends killed. Even the wife of Cartier had perished before their eyes from the onslaught of the wounded bull. Yes, the life of the People was hard, sometimes cruel.

It was no worse, however, than that of the tribes nearer civilization. There, both French and English paid bounties for enemy scalps. Since it was difficult to prove the origin of a scalp, it was suspected that some killed indiscriminately, selling scalps to the highest bidder. It was intolerable that human skin and hair had become a saleable commodity. Yes, he could understand Cartier's reluctance to expose the People to such degradation. He had to admit that for the most part, he agreed completely with the sergeant's motives. Certainly, he had overreacted when Cartier returned.

He realized that they both had arrived at the same point of appreciation for the prairie. It was a different world than they had known, completely foreign both to the civilizations of Europe and to the military frontier of New France. Despite its very harshness there was predictability, and the calming reassurance of its far horizons. There was a spirit here that he had felt nowhere else. He knew that Cartier felt much the same thing. He could understand why the tallgrass country was called by the People the "Sacred Hills." Their spirit was something that could be felt.

Perhaps this was the answer to their dilemma. Perhaps each of them had already made his decision individually. If they did nothing, then this in itself was already a decision. A decision to forsake civilization and embrace the harsh but uncomplicated and free life of the People.

No matter, they would talk of it.

He was watching toward the distant village, waiting for Cartier to appear. He had intentionally arrived early, to have some private time to think. The evening was clear and calm, with a touch of pleasant south breeze. Shadows were lengthening, and the creatures of the day were singing their last songs before turning the responsibility over to the night-creatures.

Du Pres saw a horseman in the distance, perhaps halfway between the hilltop and the village. Good. Cartier was on his way. He watched the figure.

There was something odd about the rider's behavior. He should have been riding directly toward the rendezvous on the hill. Instead, he was circling, maneuvering, staying in the ditches and gullies while he seemed to explore the terrain.

What was Cartier trying to do? The unpleasant thought crossed his mind that the sergeant intended somehow to betray his confidence, perhaps to lie in ambush.

No sooner had this thought intruded, however, than he saw another figure. This rider had started from the village and was headed straight for the hill where Du Pres sat. In an instant he recognized Cartier's bay mare.

Who, then, was the other rider? A warning began to sound in the far reaches of Du Pres's mind. Fascinated, he watched the two riders. For a time, he could not be sure whether they saw each other. Gradually, he realized that the stranger was hidden from Cartier's view.

He became more alarmed when the rider dismounted and tied his horse in concealment. The man then moved on foot along a little gully that led toward the path followed by Cartier.

Something was wrong. In the failing light of the time just before sunset, he could not be sure, but he had seen enough. He rose and sprinted to his horse, kicking the startled animal to a run down the hill.

He still did not know entirely what was happening. Someone was stalking Sergeant Cartier from ambush.

39

» » »

Cartier was deep in thought as he rode out to meet the lieutenant. He was glad when Pale Star came to him and told him that Du Pres wanted to talk.

He had done much soul-searching since, but had come to no real conclusions. He, too, had realized that both he and Du Pres were right, and both were wrong. Life had always seemed simpler when he was with the People, until now. Now, the conflict of two worlds weighed heavily on his shoulders. He suspected that the same dilemma faced Du Pres, but the lieutenant was reacting completely different.

Cartier resented that while he had been most ready to follow the rules of their military obligation, Du Pres now criticized him as a deserter. How could the lieutenant do so? Their problems were the same, and the answer must be the same for both. It was good that they were now preparing to talk. Perhaps they could plan their course of action.

He rode straight toward the hilltop, the sun in his eyes obscuring his distant view. He looked mostly at the ground a few steps in front, only occasionally lifting his eyes to make certain of his direction.

Before long, the shadow of the hill crept across the

prairie and he entered its shade. Now he could see somewhat better. He observed a lark on a stone, and watched a
great blue heron beat its way across the sky toward its
lodge in some distant rookery.

He reined his horse aside to avoid disturbing a snake
that seemed a little late in returning to its den. Strange,
the importance of the real-snake in his escape from the
warriors intent on doing him harm. He wondered for a
moment if this snake was an omen, a warning of some
sort. No, of course not, he told himself.

Cartier raised his eyes to the hilltop. He wondered if
Du Pres was already waiting there. A flash of motion
caught his eye, and he reined in to identify the rapidly
moving object.

A horseman was riding down the slope at reckless
breakneck speed. Cartier was astonished. No horseman
should take such a risk, either for himself or for his
horse. Unless, of course, in extreme emergency. The distant figure was waving his arms and yelling, and with a
shock, Cartier recognized Lieutenant Du Pres. What
could he be so excited about?

It took another moment to realize that he was yelling a
warning as he frantically waved his arms. Even then he
was slow to react. He could not think what the danger
might be.

A movement to his left caught his eye, and he reined
the horse to look that way. A man was rising from a
crouching position behind a bush, and was in the very act
of drawing his bow. It was an easy shot, too close to miss.

Cartier had no time to defend himself. He might have
thrown himself from the horse to fight on foot, but he
was caught unawares. He stiffened and gave an involun-
tary jerk on the rein. The bay mare, startled by this treat-
ment and by the unexpected appearance of the figure
behind the bush, tossed her head high in alarm.

Probably this reaction saved her rider's life but for-
feited her own. The arrow intended for Cartier struck the

mare in the throat and she fell, bleeding and choking for breath.

Cartier was fighting to kick free of the dying animal's struggles, at the same time reaching for a weapon. He had been carrying his bow and a quiver of arrows, but the bow had been broken by the fall. He grasped for the knife at his waist and did not find it. There was no time to look.

His opponent was running forward, fitting another arrow to the string. Unarmed, Cartier crouched behind the dead horse and prepared to try to dodge the missile when it came. His hand encountered his quiver and in desperation he grasped an arrow. He could hear the approaching hoofbeats of Du Pres's horse, realizing that he would not arrive in time.

The running warrior paused and the arrow flew. Cartier tried to jump aside, but the stone-tipped shaft tore through the fleshy part of his left upper arm. He had only one chance now. He leaped across the body of the horse and met the warrior in mid-stride. The arrow in his right hand swung upward in a short arc. It entered the soft part of the attacker's upper belly just beneath the ribs, ranging upward into the chest cavity.

Cartier shoved the man away and stood over him while he watched the expression in the eyes change from hate to surprise to expressionless nothing.

Du Pres came to a sliding stop and leaped from his horse, ready for action that was now unnecessary.

"Mon dieu!" he exclaimed. "Who is he?"

"His name is Black Squirrel," Cartier answered weakly. "He tried to kill my wife once."

Weakness was sweeping over him, and he sat down on the dead horse.

"You are bleeding!" exclaimed Du Pres. "Here, let me help you!"

With a jerk, he drew the arrow on through the injured flesh and tossed it aside. In moments, he was binding the arm tightly to control the bleeding, using strips cut from his own leggings.

Cartier's head was reeling, and his weakness made the descending twilight seem darker. People were running from the camp, unsure of what was happening. Du Pres helped the wounded man to lie down.

"We will bring a pole-drag, Woodchuck," he said in the tongue of the People.

"We need to talk, Lieutenant."

"No, I think not."

"Yes," Cartier insisted. "We must do the same thing. Either we both go back to Mishi-ghan, or . . ."

"Yes, I know. We can talk, Woodchuck, but I think we have both decided. We are men of the People."

Yellow Head ran up and dropped to her knees beside the prostrate form. Her husband grasped her hand. She turned to Du Pres.

"He is all right, Sky-Eyes?"

"Yes, his wound is slight. He is strong."

She turned to look at the dead man.

"Black Squirrel."

"Yes. He told me."

"Woodchuck fought for me before, Sky-Eyes."

"You have a good man."

Yellow Head smiled, and brushed a wisp of grass from her husband's face.

"Yes, I know," she said, to no one in particular.

GENEALOGY

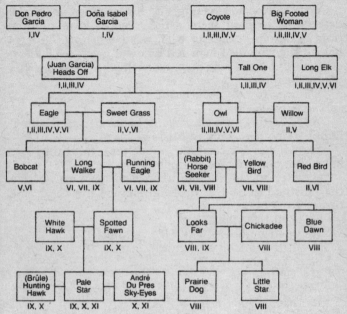

```
Don Pedro          Doña Isabel              Coyote          Big Footed
  Garcia             Garcia                                   Woman
   I,IV                I,IV              I,II,III,IV,V      I,II,III,IV,V
        │                │                    │                │
        └────────┬───────┘                    │                │
                 │                             │                │
           (Juan Garcia)                    Tall One         Long Elk
            Heads Off
           I,II,III,IV               I,II,III,IV       I,II,III,IV,V,VI
                 │                        │
        ┌────────┴──────────┐     ┌───────┴────────┐
        │                   │     │                │
      Eagle            Sweet Grass  Owl          Willow
  I,II,III,IV,V,VI       II,V,VI   II,III,IV,V,VI   II,V
        │                             │
  ┌─────┼──────┐           ┌──────────┼──────────┐
  │     │      │           │          │          │
Bobcat  Long  Running   (Rabbit)    Yellow    Red Bird
        Walker  Eagle   Horse Seeker  Bird
  V,VI  VI,VII,IX VI,VII,IX VI,VII,VIII VII,VIII   II,VI
           │                  │
     ┌─────┴─────┐       ┌─────┴──────┐
     │           │       │            │
  White       Spotted  Looks       Chickadee    Blue
  Hawk         Fawn     Far                      Dawn
  IX,X         IX,X    VIII,IX       VIII        VIII
     │                    │
 ┌───┴────┬──────────┐   ┌┴──────────┐
 │        │          │   │           │
(Brûle)  Pale    André  Prairie    Little
Hunting  Star    Du Pres  Dog       Star
Hawk             Sky-Eyes
IX,X   IX,X,XI   X,XI    VIII        VIII
```

Dates for Volumes in the Spanish Bit Saga

I	TRAIL OF THE SPANISH BIT	— 1540-44
II	THE ELK-DOG HERITAGE	— 1544-45
III	FOLLOW THE WIND	— 1547-48
IV	BUFFALO MEDICINE	— 1559-61
V	MAN OF THE SHADOWS	— 1565-66
VI	DAUGHTER OF THE EAGLE	— 1583-84
VII	THE MOON OF THUNDER	— 1600-01
VIII	THE SACRED HILLS	— 1625-27
IX	PALE STAR	— 1630-31
X	RIVER OF SWANS	— 1636-38
XI	RETURN TO THE RIVER	— 1642-44

Dates are only approximate, since the People have no written calendar.
Characters in the Genealogy appear in the volumes indicated.

About the Author

» » »

DON COLDSMITH was born in Iola, Kansas, in 1926. He served as a World War II combat medic in the South Pacific and returned to his native state where he graduated from Baker University in 1949 and received his M.D. from the University of Kansas in 1958. He worked at several jobs before entering medical school: he was a YMCA group counselor, a gunsmith, a taxidermist, and, for a short time, a Congregational preacher. In addition to his private medical practice, Dr. Coldsmith is a staff physician at Emporia State University's Health Center, teaches in the English Department, and is active as a free-lance writer, lecturer, and rancher. He and his wife of 26 years, Edna, have raised five daughters.

Dr. Coldsmith produced the first ten novels in "The Spanish Bit Saga" in a five-year period; he writes and revises the stories first in his head, then in longhand. From this manuscript he reads aloud to his wife, whom he calls his "chief editor." Finally the finished version is skillfully typed by his longtime office receptionist.

Of his decision to create, or re-create, the world of the Plains Indian in the 16th and 17th centuries, the author says: "There has been very little written about this time period. I wanted also to portray these Native Americans as human beings, rather than as stereotyped 'Indians.' That word does not appear anywhere in the series—for a reason. As I have researched the time and place, the indigenous cultures, it's been a truly inspiring experience for me."